KISS

FOR

A

KILLER

ALSO BY G. G. FICKLING

This Girl for Hire

KISS FOR A KILLER

G. G. Fickling

THE OVERLOOK PRESS
Woodstock · New York

This edition first published in paperback in the United States in 2006 by
The Overlook Press, Peter Mayer Publishers, Inc.
New York & Woodstock

NEW YORK:
141 Wooster Street
New York, NY 10012

WOODSTOCK:
One Overlook Drive
Woodstock, NY 12498
www.overlookpress.com
[for individual orders, bulk and special sales, contact our Woodstock office]

Copyright © 1960 by Gloria and Forrest E. Fickling

All Rights Reserved. No part of this publication may be reproduced or
transmitted in any form or by any means, electronic or mechanical, including
photocopy, recording, or any information storage and retrieval system now
known or to be invented without permission in writing from the publisher,
except by a reviewer who wishes to quote brief passages in connection with
a review written for inclusion in a magazine, newspaper, or broadcast.

Originally published in 1960 by Pyramid Books

Cataloging-in-Publication Data is available from the Library of Congress

Book design and type formatting by Bernard Schleifer
Manufactured in Canada
FIRST EDITION
ISBN 1-58567-758-2
1 3 5 7 9 8 6 4 2

KISS FOR A KILLER

ONE

"**H**oney?" The telephone receiver crackled in my ear. I glared into the neon glow across the alley, barely recognizing Lieutenant Mark Storm's voice through the wail of sirens wedged behind his words. Fog lay deep over the city, cutting its lights and buildings into squalid slits.

"What's the matter, Lieutenant?"

"Plenty!" he continued, his voice tight, like the voice of a man who's just seen something he wished he hadn't. "Plenty, dammit! Do you know an L.A. Rams football player named Rip Spensor?"

"Sure," I said, flicking wet blonde hair from my eyes as I bent over a cigarette box. I was just out of my office shower and sporting a few goose pimples and a towel. "Rip and I go out together occasionally. Why?"

"You've had your last date," the deputy said harshly. "He's dead."

"What?"

"I understand he was six-foot-six. He ain't any more, Honey," the voice managed. "Brace yourself for a shock. Somebody ran him over with a steam roller!"

That picture splattered in my mind and I jerked upright, cigarette sliding from my mouth. "Mark, you're kidding!"

"I wish I were," the big man from Sheriff's Homicide blared. "He lives south of the Coliseum in county territory. They're improving the road in front of his house. He was ground right into the asphalt."

I pictured the heavy-jawed face of Rip Spensor, a handsome young guy off the campus of Notre Dame, big, powerful, sleek, and worth a million dollars to the professional Los Angeles Rams. I'd known Rip only three months, watched him toss touchdown passes in practice at Riverside, felt those same strong arms draw me against him.

"When'd this happen, Mark?" I asked incredulously. "About two hours ago." Sirens still wailed behind his voice. I could also hear the metallic clang of a huge construction machine. "I wouldn't have called you, Honey, except when we started going over his house we found your picture on the table next to his bed. Framed in a big heart."

"My picture?"

"That's right." His tone sharpened. "You do all right, don't you, sweetheart? What are you running these days, a detective agency or a lonely hearts club?"

"Now look, Lieutenant, I knew Rip Spensor. That's all. I didn't realize he felt that—that deeply about me."

Mark groaned angrily. "For an eyeball you don't know much, do you? For instance, he played against the San Francisco Forty-niners tonight at the Coliseum. Were you there? I tried to reach you earlier at your apartment."

"No, I—"

"He ran ninety-six yards for a touchdown and you didn't even listen to the radio broadcast?"

"No, I was catching a late catnap here at my office. I told you, Lieutenant, this was strictly a friendly relationship, and that's all. Now take out your green teeth. You're biting hunks out of me."

"I'd like nothing better."

Mark Storm was an irrepressible six-foot-five-inch hunk of habitual hound dog. He never stopped making passes at me.

"Where are you?" I said, brushing the towel down over my dripping legs.

"A hundred and eighty-second off Figueroa. Aren't you familiar with the address?"

"No!"

"Foggy as hell out here, Honey. The ambulance just came in from County Local. So did a crew from the construction gang."

"I'm coming out, Mark."

"It's quarter-past two in the morning," he returned sarcastically. "You'd better get your beauty sleep, lover girl."

"I've had my usual," I said, retrieving my cigarette and touching a match to it.

"Come out if you want, but don't expect to keep your dinner down. I didn't."

"Mark, is it really that bad?"

He paused before answering, the harsh clatter of steel against steel ringing in the background. "It's worse, Honey."

"You certain it wasn't an accident?"

"Are you kidding?" he said. "Since when does a three-ton steam roller run amuck all by itself on a flat road?"

"Any suspects, Mark?"

"A cousin named Ray Spensor who shared this house. He's also with the Rams. And a couple of others."

"Okay," I said. "I'll be there in about thirty minutes."

I hung up, towelled myself off and stubbed out my cigarette. Fog nestled over the neon across the alley, wetly clawing at the dark sky and at the distant lights of the Pike and harbor. I slipped into a pair of panties and a bra, then encircled my right thigh with a garter holster and inserted my pearl-handled .22 before getting into a blue cashmere sweater and skirt. The clamor of the Pike's merry-go-round and roller coaster was stilled now in the late-night darkness and fog. The horn of a ship trapped somewhere in Long Beach Harbor moaned faintly.

The terrible image of Rip Spensor being mangled on a wet road kept clicking through my brain like old-fashioned slides in a penny arcade picture machine. Each frame was more ghastly than the last. The ponderous steam roller wheezing and clanking on the asphalt. The steel cylinder suddenly rearing out of the fog. Knocking

Rip down. Crushing over him as if he were an ant.

My convertible was parked in an alley behind the office building. Fog swirled up into my face as I moved toward the car. So did the sound of someone running on the hard asphalt. I flattened against a brick wall, snapping the revolver out from beneath my skirt. The steps were hard, slamming quickly in heavy, mannish strides. They were moving toward Third Street and away from me. After an instant, I started in the same direction, but the sound of something metal falling in the alley stopped me again. It bounced several times, then rolled against a wall a few feet from the corner. The footsteps died.

A bus's gears clashed and a yellow Metropolitan whirled past the alley, its headlights winking in the mist. I guessed the mysterious runner had either climbed aboard the bus or made it to a car along Third. Either way he was gone. I tucked my revolver back into its holster and advanced toward the shadowed outline of what looked like a large tin can. I was fairly certain he'd dropped the container and not just accidentally kicked it in his flight.

The can was a coffee tin, punctured on top with numerous air holes as though to house some kind of living creature. Bits of dirt poured from the openings as I examined it in the faint glow of a street light that cut through the fog. Carefully, I pried the lid open. Except for some dried soil clinging to the shiny metal, there was nothing inside. I tucked the can under my arm and walked back to the convertible, hoping a sharper light might reveal something more.

Inside the car I flicked on a small dash light, then got the mobile operator on my auto phone. After reaching my office number, the answering service cut in gruffly.

"H. West, private investigations, whatta you want at this hour?"

"Whatta you think?" I retorted. "A polite, cultured, romantic voice. When are you going to break down and hire one, Charley?"

"What's the matter with my voice, Springtime? I'll have you know I won a speech contest when I was twelve."

"Where was that, at the zoo?"

He groaned. Charley April had a groan that was indefinable. So was the rest of him. He weighed over three hundred pounds and was a perfect blend of beer, bear and bombast. Why I kept him for my answering service was definable. He never sent me a bill. My line and some other chosen few were used as a front for a bookie operation he ran from his broken-down switchboard. But Charley was harmless. Despite the fact that he worked outside the limits of the law, nobody, including Lieutenant Marcus Storm, could bring themselves to close him up. Charley gave more money to polio, cancer and crippled children's funds than a dozen legitimate millionaires all rolled into one. And he talked more horse players out of horsing around with the ponies than he took bets. Where he got all his money from, nobody knew, or asked. Charley April was just that kind of guy.

"Look, Charley! I'm in the alley behind my office. I have a hunch some character was just casing me, my car, or both. I want you to do me a favor."

"No, thanks," he said quickly. "I ain't good in alleys. They're not wide enough for me. Besides I'm casing a case right now of my own."

"I can imagine," I said, picturing him bent over his switchboard with a bottle of beer jammed under my office key. "I want you to refer any calls for me in the next hour to my auto phone. I'm going out to a Hundred and eighty-second and Figueroa. A football player's been murdered out there."

"What? Listen, Springtime. You're a nice girl. Blonde hair. Blue eyes. Baby-bottom complexion. Why don't you quit while they're still all in one piece. I worry about you."

"Thanks, Charley. I worry about you, too."

"Why?" he drawled in that inimitable beer-barrel voice. "I ain't worth much."

I had to smile. "You won a speech contest once, didn't you? That's worth something, isn't it?"

The buttons were probably busting on his sweaty old shirt when he answered. "Oh, I guess so. But, now you keep your nose clean, understand. I don't want nobody saying they knew you when."

"I'll talk to you later, Charley. Meanwhile, don't let the bugs bite."

"What bugs?"

"The kind that come in those cases you said you're casing. Good night, Charley."

"Good night, Springtime."

He clicked off. I jammed down on the starter and my convertible's engine growled dismally in the damp night. I repeated the action. Suddenly it kicked over and roared up into an 8-cylinder symphony of tappets and valves. That's when I jammed down on something else. I peered through the glare of the dash light and felt a scream welling up in my throat.

A bug squatted beneath my foot. It was about as big as any I'd ever seen in my life. It was thick and black and its legs spread frighteningly huge on the rubber mat. Hair stemmed from its ugly body.

I jerked backward, allowing the mammoth spider to dart out from beneath my heel, and whirled toward the door handle nearest me. My hand touched something soft and warm and awesome. I recoiled, feeling pain stab up my arm.

In the faint grim light I saw another one clinging to the back of my hand. Then it dropped in my lap, legs spinning.

TWO

The sound that erupted in my throat was loud and twisted.

I swung wildly with my elbow, brushing the spider from my lap.

In the misty glow of neon slanting from across the alley another of the horrifying creatures glinted into view. It crawled down the back of the seat, hairy legs radiating grotesquely from around its thick body. I straightened, snatched my revolver from its holster and dropped the gun butt on the spider. It flattened on the seat, then arched up again, legs flicking wildly, and lunged at me. I fell back against the seat, grabbed madly at the door handle. Another spider leaped onto my shoulder.

I screamed again, tumbling into the fog-shrouded alley. My head struck asphalt. . . .

When I woke up, I was in Mark Storm's office at Sheriff's Homicide. The big lieutenant bent over me.

"You all right, Honey?"

"I—I think so. What—what happened?"

"A couple of patrolmen found you in the alley behind your office. Your car was crawling with tarantulas. Charley April says you called him about some guy casing the area."

I listened to the sound of water dripping outside his window. It was running down off the eaves and striking a tin roof below. A fog horn still blared far out in the bay. I told Mark the story. What I knew. The tin can. The sudden sensation under my foot, like a mouse.

"They were huge, Mark," I shuddered.

"So I noticed. Hector's got a couple of them in the lab right now. He's checking to see what variety they are."

He removed his peacock-blue felt hat and rubbed dampness from the crown, then tossed it on his desk. After a moment, he looked at me again. I was lying on a couch in one corner of his office. My right hand hurt. It was bandaged.

He tucked a cigarette in his broad mouth and asked, "Did you see the man?"

"No. Aren't tarantulas supposed to be nonpoisonous, Mark?"

He winced, lit a match and inhaled some smoke. "They used to say in South America that the bite of a tarantula created an insane desire to dance. I guess that's how the Cha-Cha-Cha became popular. How you doing?"

"All I've got is an itch."

"Where?"

"On my hand, Lieutenant. By the way, who performed the first aid?"

"Doc Carter. The only swelling and perforations he could find were on the back of that hand. Honey, how do you manage to get into so much trouble in such a short time?"

"I practice. With Arthur Murray tarantulas. What time is it?"

He studied his watch. "Quarter to four. Fog's still pea soup thick." He sat on the edge of his desk and rubbed his big hands together. "I just got back from the morgue. Spensor's a mess. Do you think there's any connection?"

"Between what?"

"Between the steam roller and the tarantulas."

I sat up slowly, brushing hair from my eyes. "Maybe."

Mark moved to the window, peering out between two of the plastic slats. "You sure it was a man?"

"Sounded like one. Heavy. Not brittle like high heels or light like a woman's flats."

He rubbed at his forehead. "There's another woman in this case."

"What do you mean, *another?*"

"Besides you."

I stood up, the pain in my hand increasing as I moved. "How do I fit?"

"The photograph of you next to Spensor's bed." He fixed taut brown eyes on me. "Was this serious?"

"I told you, no, Mark."

He brought his fist down hard on the desk. "You're a smart apple, aren't you, Honey?"

"You always called me a peach, Lieutenant."

"Don't be funny. What if those babies had been black widows?"

"Then Rip Spensor and I could have shared the same slab."

"Yeah, just like you've shared a few other things."

"Lieutenant, your mind is positively one-track."

"You're the one who's one-track," he thundered. "That license of yours ought to be hanging over a four-poster. You don't solve cases, you entertain them!"

Hector Gonzales, a thin, bespectacled lab man, came into the room, carrying a paper in his hand. His swarthy face was haggard and his hands shook nervously as he stared at us.

"Those are Mygales," he said flatly.

"What?" the deputy boomed.

"Mygales," Hector repeated carefully. "The technical name is Theraphosidae, a species of trap-door spider. The largest of any known living species. Stout, dark brown or black in color, thick legs covered with hair mingled with longer bristles—"

"Don't give us all that crap, Hector," Mark returned hotly. "Are they dangerous?"

"Yes."

"How dangerous?"

"We let one of them loose with a white rat. He was dead in thirty seconds. With convulsions. They have been known to kill large birds."

Mark's eyes flicked at me. "How about people?"

Hector squinted through his glasses. "On occasion, if the venom is injected into the right spot. Miss West was apparently fortunate. The back of the hand is not a very vulnerable area."

I smiled faintly, rubbing the injured hand. "Well, Lieutenant, what were we saying about the entertaining qualities of my job?"

His big face reddened. "All right, I apologize, but you have no right to be meddling in this case."

"Rip kept a photograph of me that says I do," I countered. "May I go now?"

"Sure," Mark said grimly, not looking at me. "Your car's parked downstairs. It's been thoroughly cleaned out, so don't worry."

I started toward the door. "I won't."

He moved in front of me, blocking my path with his six-foot-five frame. "Only let me give you a word of advice. There are all kinds of spiders. So watch out."

"What kind did you have in mind, Lieutenant?"

"The female of the species," he said. "The other woman."

"Who is she?"

"Angela Scali."

I frowned. "The Italian Angel?"

"That's right. This year's Academy Award winner. Hollywood's answer to the H-bomb."

"But, Mark, she disappeared months ago."

"Right again. She may be dead, and then again—"

"How do you know she was involved with Rip Spensor?"

Mark exhaled smoke at the ceiling and scratched his ear thoughtfully. "I'll let you figure that out."

"Okay, I will."

I pushed him out of the way, but he caught my arm.

"One other thing, Miss Sexiest-Private-Eye."

"What's that?"

"In Spensor's wallet, we found a card stating his membership in some sort of health cult operated by a man named Thor Tunny. Do you have any information about this organization?"

"Maybe."

"I want the address of Tunny's headquarters."

"The dues are too high for you, Lieutenant."

He gripped my arm. "I'm serious, Honey."

"San Berdoo Mountains, I don't know the exact location." I stepped around him. "Now, if you don't mind I've got some entertaining to do."

The big deputy's jaw tightened and he let me go. "Okay," he said. "Be smart. Only one of these days you'll wind up in the same gutter as your father."

"Thanks for the warning," I said. "I'll take it up with my four-poster."

The corridor outside Mark's office was thick with shadows crawling along the ceiling and walls like diabolical monsters lying in wait for my exit. My heels clattered on the stairway, striking hollowly on the steel treads. Outside the building, the fog had degenerated into a moist film that chilled my face. My car was parked near the corner in a special lot for Sheriff's vehicles. An officer on duty gave me the keys. I climbed behind the wheel, shuddering at the memory of my last contact with the convertible, and started the engine.

A block away from the Sheriff's office, the haze lifted

slightly and I was able to increase my speed. For an instant I thought I noticed a pair of headlights flicker in my rear view mirror as I turned onto Pacific Coast highway, but my mind was too tightly fixed on what Mark had been saying to check whether I was being followed. I couldn't get over the fact Rip Spensor had been a member of Thor Tunny's health cult. He'd never divulged such a connection to me. I didn't know too much about Tunny's cult, but what I knew was pretty sickening.

I called my office on the auto phone. Charley cut in abruptly.

"Yes, Springtime."

"How'd you know it was me, Charley?"

"I just talked with Lieutenant Storm at Homicide. He said you'd left. You okay?"

"Sure," I said. "Only one of those creatures I warned you about bit me."

"So I understand. There was a call for you about a half-hour ago."

"Who was it, Charley?"

"Pardon the expression, but that's what bugs me."

"What do you mean?"

"It was long distance. That much I got. The party refused to give her name."

"Her?"

"Yeah, it was a dame, Springtime. She had a nice voice. Real sexy, if you know what I mean."

"How sexy, Charley?"

"Husky. Like she was going to eat me or something."

"What'd she say?"

"She said she wanted to speak to you, natch. I said you were sort of incapacitated since I'd heard from Lieutenant Storm about the terantulers in your car."

"What else?" I asked.

"That's it, Springtime. She hung up. But I got the operator."

"Good boy, Charley. Where was the call from?"

"Meadow Falls."

"Where's that?"

"The operator was intercepting from Long Beach. She said the call came from a trunk line located near San Berdoo. Does that help any?"

"It sure does. Thanks."

"That's okay, Springtime, only you'd better be more careful."

"I'm trying, Charley. Now you'd better get some sleep."

He grumbled in that way that meant he wished he didn't weigh three hundred pounds plus and was twenty years younger.

"Hell, Honey, sleep's what I don't need. I'll get plenty of that when I'm dead."

Anaheim street rolled into view as I swung off the Long Beach Freeway.

"Charley, you're a long way from dead."

"Maybe I am, but you're not."

I laughed. "Mark Storm told me the same thing. You two ought to be insurance salesmen. You both make life sound so comfy and cozy."

"I'm not joking, Honey. Where you heading?"

"None of your business."

"My business is your business. Now level with me."

As I passed a lumber company on the other side of the Anaheim bridge, a car pulled alongside me in the fog. Then it darted ahead, swerving dangerously in front of my convertible.

"Okay, I'll level," I said into the receiver. "Somebody wants to check my driver's license and I'm pretty sure it isn't a cop. I'm just beyond the river bridge on Anaheim."

"Got you, Honey," Charley said. "I'll be back in a minute." He clicked off.

I dropped the phone into its bracket and tried to speed up around the other car. It swerved into me, glancing off my front left fender, skidding across the street and back again.

I reached for my revolver, but discovered the pearl-handled .22 was gone from my holster. Mark's deputies had probably confiscated it when they found me in the alley.

The other car zoomed forward, nosed hard in front of me and skidded to a stop. I had to brake quickly to avoid a collision.

Then a weird thing happened. For a moment I thought I was having hallucinations. A man climbed from the other vehicle and stood in my headlights. He was tall and deceptively thin, and despite the fog, I could see he was ruggedly handsome. He was stark staring naked.

He moved to my side window and knocked at the glass "Open up, Miss West, quickly. It's a matter of life or death."

"Are you crazy?" I blared. "You nearly ran me off the road. And you're—"

"I know," he returned. "I'm not wearing any clothes. Open up before somebody comes along."

He wasn't carrying a weapon and his voice did sound desperate, so I flicked the lock button on my door and swung it open. He climbed in swiftly, shoving me over with a bronzed, heavily-muscled hip.

I switched on my dash light and examined his face in its faint glow. He had blue eyes and a nicely tapered nose. His hair was thick and black and slanted wetly on his broad forehead.

"Thanks," he said, breathing deeply.

"Thanks for what?" I said. "Road blocking and indecent exposure are two serious crimes in these parts. Don't tell me you lost your clothes in a poker game."

He grinned broadly. It was a nice grin, very wide and drawn loosely over straight white teeth. "I'm sorry about running you off the road. As far as clothes are concerned. I never wear them. It's against my religion."

"You—you're a nudist?"

He shook his head. "No, I'm one of Tunny's disciples. A Sun Soul."

I ran my fingers across my lips in embarrassment. "You mean you never wear clothes?"

"Never," he said abruptly. "Please, you've got to help us."

"Us?"

"Mr. Tunny and myself. We're in serious trouble."

I couldn't help glancing down at his powerfully built, muscular frame. "You're telling me. You couldn't be talking about a member of your group named Rip Spensor, could you?"

"Ex-member," he said. "Rip was expelled from the organization months ago."

"Why?"

"I can't tell you that now." His forehead ridged. "The only thing that's important is that Rip's dead."

"How'd you know?"

"A late news bulletin over the radio." He leaned toward me, one hand resting on the seat, the other brushing back a shock of black hair. "My name's Adam. Adam Jason. I'm Director of Inter-Relations and Sports at Meadow Falls."

"Meadow Falls?" I said, remembering the phone call Charley had intercepted earlier.

"Back of Lake Arrowhead in the San Bernardino Mountains. We have several acres of land. Our own temple and living quarters. It's quite new and modern."

Adam Jason was a big man, like Mark Storm, and broad-shouldered. His startling blue eyes were deep-set in his sun-burnt face. Suddenly he leaned forward and pressed his lips to my mouth.

"Hey," I said, drawing back. "What's that for?"

"I'm a director," he said. "In our cult a director's kiss is like a blessing. It is not holy for a director to speak with a female who has not been blessed."

A car flashed by on the street, its headlights winking in the mist.

"Well, you'd better count your blessings, mister," I said, "because the police'll be here in a few minutes."

"But, Miss West," he stammered. "We want to hire you."

"For what, as a blessing in disguise?"

He put his hands on my shoulders. "I'm serious. Rip Spensor's death may ruin Mr. Tunny's organization."

"Why?"

"I can't explain now, but I've been authorized by Mr. Tunny to bring you back to Meadow Falls. He'll go into detail. We're willing to pay any reasonable price for your services."

"Why me?" I demanded. "There must be fifty-odd private investigators in Southern California to choose from. How'd you pick my name? Certainly not out of your hat."

"You were acquainted with Rip," he said quickly.

"Where'd you get this information?"

"When Rip joined our organization he was asked to give some references. Your name was at the head of the list, along with your occupation."

"So?"

"So Mr. Tunny picked you because of your obvious association with the deceased. He asked that you be returned to Meadow Falls."

"What if I'm not interested?"

He straightened. "You've got to be!"

"Why?"

"I said before it's a matter of life or death."

I shrugged. "Rip Spensor's already dead, Mr. Jason. Who else did you have in mind?"

His jaw tightened grimly. "You, Miss West."

THREE

"Me?" I demanded. "Now look, Nature Boy, in less than five minutes, you've bent my fender, my ear, my morals, and now you're trying to bend my life span. Don't threaten me!"

"I'm not trying to threaten you," he countered. "I'm trying to help. That's why I followed you from the Sheriff's office."

"You didn't happen to follow me into an alley a couple of hours ago, did you?" I glanced down at his feet, but it was too dark to see whether he was wearing shoes.

His face flushed. "I'm not in the habit of lurking in dark alleys, Miss West."

"How'd you know it was dark?"

"I don't even know what you're talking about, but if it was only a few hours ago the alley must have been dark—and foggy." He threw his head back and exhaled audibly. "Please, Miss West. Are you going to take the case, or aren't you?"

"I've got to think about it," I said. "But not here. We'd better go to my office."

I took a car blanket from the rear seat and tossed it in his lap. "Here. Wrap yourself up until we get there. I've got some old clothes of my father's that should fit you."

He shook his head vigorously. "I never wear them, Miss West, it's against my—"

"—religion. You told me." I examined him carefully. "But, how are we going to get any work done with you parading around in nothing but a healthy suntan?"

He leaned toward me again. "Miss West—"

"Down, tiger. You'll wear clothes or else."

"Or else what?"

"Or else the deal's off."

He shrugged, wrapped the blanket around his thick shoulders and said, "I wish you belonged to our organization, Miss West. You're a very attractive woman."

"I'm not the organization type, Mr. Jason. Besides, when I take my clothes off it's for one reason, and one reason only."

His eyes lighted. "What's that?"

"To take a shower." My eyes shifted to the street. "Your car's far enough off the road. We'll leave it here temporarily."

I got out on the passenger side and walked around. The fog was thinning now and street lights beyond the Anaheim bridge were beginning to show through. Beyond, in the river bed, crickets chattered rhythmically. The damage to my left fender was minor. The damage to my disposition wasn't. Nothing added up. How did this nude cultist know I was at the Sheriff's office? I climbed in behind the wheel and flicked the starter.

Before we reached my office, Mark Storm had me on the auto phone.

"What's up?" the deputy demanded. "Charley says you're in trouble again."

"Not yet," I said. "But I've got a passenger."

"Not more tarantulas?"

"No," I answered lightly, shifting my gaze at Adam Jason. "This one's got two legs."

"A man?" Mark said,

"Of that there is no doubt, Lieutenant. Now be a good boy and go to bed."

"Is that where you're off to, Miss Four Poster?"

"Lieutenant, you don't quit, do you? This man's a possible client."

"For what?"

"For the Rip Spensor case. Now are you satisfied?"

"No!" Mark bellowed. "You stay away from the Spensor case. It's hot."

"Not as hot as my client. Bye-bye, black sheep."

I hung up, turned off down Pine and parked in a lot behind my office building. Fortunately no one was on duty that time of night. I slipped Adam Jason behind a fence and got him as far as the alley before we ran smack into trouble. A patrol car turned in off Third just as we started across the alley toward the back door. A turret light swung on us like a spotlight on a couple of actors, splashing us silly with a circle of intensely brilliant light. We made the alley door, but before I could produce my key the car whirled in tight behind us.

"What's going on?" the patrolman behind the wheel shouted.

His assistant came after us with a pistol cocked at Adam, shoes smacking hard on the asphalt. "Hey, what's with the blanket?"

"He's an Indian," I said.

"There's something a little too cute about both of you," the man behind the wheel said. "You're under arrest for suspicion of breaking and entering."

"Now wait a minute," I protested. "I've got an office in this building. And a key to this door."

"Sure you have," the officer with the gun said. "And my Aunt Fanny's got a hollow left leg. Come on."

"Look," I said, producing the key. "I'll prove it."

I inserted the key in the lock and twisted it open quickly. Then before either policeman could make a move, I shoved Adam inside, handing him my purse.

"Upstairs," I said. "Room 304. The trunk is in the corner."

Adam got the message without any trouble. He stepped inside and slammed the door locked. I dropped the building key into my bra before the man with the gun could reach me or the door.

"What the hell have you done, lady?" he demanded, jerking at the handle.

"My Indian chief has a pipe of peace he's in a hurry to smoke," I said glibly. "Now why don't you gentlemen break out your own corn cobs and leave us alone."

The officer stepped out of the squad car angrily.

"Gimme that key! That guy didn't have any clothes on!"

"Prove it," I said.

"I'll prove both of you into a nice tight little cell," he snarled, pushing his partner out of the way. He advanced on me, hands lifted. "Gimme that key!"

"You touch me," I said, "and you'll wind up with a pogo stick patrolling the Pike."

He stopped, face reddening. "What's your name?"

"Honey West."

He pushed his flashlight in my face, then groaned. "I shoulda known. Get back in the car, Pete." He flicked his eyes on me witheringly. "Okay, you win this time, Miss West. Only remember this. Next time, don't act so cute with me or, pogo stick or not, I just might pinch you for the hell of it. Get me?"

I nodded. "I'll take the warning from whence it comes."

They climbed back into the squad car, the one man still grumbling and drove off. I waited a few seconds until they were out of sight in the fog and produced the key again. My third floor office door was partially open when I approached in the dark corridor. There was no light, except for a small glow at the end of the hall indicating a fire escape.

"Adam," I called. "Are you there?"

"Yes, Miss West."

"The police have gone. I hope you've got clothes on."

"I do."

I moved inside the office and switched on a desk lamp, then burst into a roar of laughter. He was standing near the door, one of my sweaters draped around his shoulders, a partially zipped skirt hanging around his bronzed hips.

He cast a chagrined look at his outfit and said, "I couldn't find the trunk."

"Adam, you take the proverbial cake," I said, shaking my head. "What if the police had come up here?"

"I don't know." His thick eyebrows lifted perplexedly. "I guess I'd have introduced myself as a female impersonator."

"With your build?"

He shrugged, nearly losing my skirt.

I crossed to my father's old trunk, pulled out a pair of pants and a shirt and handed them to him.

"There's a screen behind you," I said. "Try these for size. They're apt to be a better fit."

He went behind the screen and tossed my sweater over the top. "You've sure got a narrow waist for such a big girl."

"Five-feet-five, isn't so big," I said. "That's in my stocking feet."

"I didn't mean length, I meant breadth!"

"I weigh a hundred and twenty pounds, Mr. Jason. Thirty-eight, twenty-two, thirty-six. Something wrong with that?"

"Are you kidding, Honey? Is it all right if I call you Honey? It sounds so—so intimate."

"Hardly more intimate than you've been in the past hour," I said, taking a cigarette from a box on the desk. "Why don't you fill me in on Rip Spensor."

"All right." My skirt sailed over the screen, landing

on the floor. "I played ball with Rip at Notre Dame. He was a great guy. Terrific ball hawk. Good passer."

"He was that," I said, recalling some of our dates.

"Rip went professional," Adam continued. "I didn't. When I got out of college I wanted something more substantial. A goal. You know what I mean?"

"Is that how you met Tunny?"

"Sort of. Hey, your dad must be a pretty big guy."

"He was," I said, "until somebody put a bullet in his back."

"He's dead?"

"Five years," I said, exhaling smoke through my nostrils. "It was raining that night. Somebody ambushed him in an alley behind the Paramount Theatre in L.A."

"Gee, I'm sorry."

"Me, too," I said. "He was a fine man. This was his office before he died."

"You mean you took up where he left off?"

"Sort of," I said, staring at the fog and neon across the alley. "I've tried for years to find who murdered him. I haven't been successful yet."

"You've got a lot of guts, Honey."

I smiled faintly. "So the officer said downstairs."

Adam came from behind the screen. Wearing his clothes, he looked a lot like my dad, tall, rangy, full-shouldered. I couldn't help saying it.

"I like you, Adam."

"Does that mean you'll take the case?"

"I guess that's what it means," I said, rubbing my bandaged hand. "Sometimes I wonder why I keep this office. I seem to get into more trouble than I get people out of."

"I hope you can help me, Honey."

"Spell it out for me, Adam."

He hitched up his pants and shot a forlorn look at his awkwardly big hands. "I got into a fight with Rip last week. Up at the camp."

"Who started it?"

"He did," Adam said dismally. "He came up to collect some money Mr. Tunny owed him for helping with the summer athletic program. Rip said it wasn't enough and started pushing Mr. Tunny around. So I grabbed him and he swung on me."

"That doesn't sound like Rip, Adam."

"I'll go along with that. He flattened me twice. The third time around, he got it back in spades. I gave him a hard right uppercut and he dropped like a bomb. He said he'd kill me if he ever got the chance. I was really burning. I told him he wouldn't kill me if I got him first."

"No doubt several people overheard these remarks."

"Several?" he blurted, shoulders sagging dismally. "Practically the entire congregation. When the police find out we had a fight and I threatened Rip's life, they're going to have me by the seat of my pants."

"What pants?"

"You know what I mean!"

"You're clean unless you were driving that steam roller."

"I had nothing to do with that!"

I tore the bandage from my hand and crossed into the bathroom. "Have you ever met a gal named Angela Scali?"

"The movie actress?"

"Yes. The Italian Angel."

He rubbed at his nose thoughtfully. "I've seen her in pictures. Never met her personally."

"Why'd you hesitate before answering, Adam?"

"Just tired I guess."

I ran cold water over the swelling and rebandaged my hand, using a small triangle of gauze this time to cover the area. When I was finished, I came back into the room and examined Adam cautiously. He was wearing thick-soled shoes. The kind that make a lot of noise when they slam against asphalt.

After a moment, I asked, "How long would it take us to get to Meadow Falls?"

"Little over two hours." His eyebrows lifted. "You're not thinking about going now, are you?"

"Of course not."

In my desk was a file on Thor Tunny's nude health cult. I knew more about the organization than Adam realized. A woman had hired me several weeks earlier to find her daughter. Twelve hours later the young girl had turned up at home, whitefaced and trembling. She had gone up to Lake Arrowhead for a weekend with some of her sorority sisters. While at the mountain resort she'd met Tunny and he'd talked her into joining his group. Being over twenty-one, she signed a legal agreement stating she'd work for the organization in return for the cost of any monthly dues. Then they stripped off her clothes and initiated her into the cult. She escaped that same night. She was too frightened and ashamed to tell the entire story. But it added up to sexual abuse carried out in a subterranean room accompanied by the weird howl of music and flickering orange lights.

"Adam, I've heard some very bad things about Tunny and his health cult."

His jaws tightened. "Whatever you've heard, Honey, it's nothing but vicious scandal. All lies."

"I doubt that," I said, "but I'm willing to see for myself." I drew the screen back and indicated a couch in the corner. "You can curl up here."

"Where are you going to sleep?"

"I've an apartment near Alamitos Bay. I'll call you about ten, okay?"

He nodded. "Do I have to sleep with these clothes on?"

"I don't care how you sleep," I said. "Just be dressed when I come to pick you up, understand. Another run-in like we had a few minutes ago and you'll wind up skinned. And that's no joke."

"Okay." He yawned, stretched and flicked a broad smile at me. "Thanks, Honey. You won't regret this."

"I hope not," I said, crossing to the office door.

I switched off the light, checked the lock and listened to it click as I closed the glass-paneled door. Halfway down the corridor, I got the feeling I was being watched. I glanced back at my office, but the door remained closed. On the back stairway I felt the chill of the fog and noticed the building's rear door was open. Had I forgotten to close it earlier in my haste? The door banged gently, pushed by a pre-dawn breeze which had lifted off the ocean. I stopped on the bottom step and watched it swing erratically back and forth. From where

I stood I could see the parking lot across the alley.

Suddenly something poked me in the back. It felt hard, like the muzzle of a gun.

"Anyone for tarantulas?" a voice demanded.

I whirled. On the step above me stood a gaunt, slightly bent figure, clutching a cane. His steel-grey eyes looked down at me, the whites glinting in the dim light.

"Fred Sims," I said angrily. "You're lucky I'm not carrying a gun."

He laughed sourly, lowering his cane. "You're darn right I am. I wouldn't have tried that if I weren't certain. Here!"

He tossed me my pearl-handled .22. "Lieutenant Storm sends it with his compliments."

Fred Sims was a reporter for the Long Beach *Press-Telegram*. For a man with a crippled leg he got around faster than the seven-year-itch. Our friendship spanned the same number of years with about as many complications. He was a hard-hearted guy with more guts and gumption than a Missouri mule. Which is what he acted like at Bastogne during World War II. He had half a leg to prove it. Also a Congressional Medal of Honor. And a face that never smiled unless it was watching an execution.

"How'd you get in here?" I asked, putting the gun into my garter holster.

"How do you think?" he said. "I blew the door open with dynamite. Now what's the story on you and Thor Tunny?"

"He and I go steady," I said, adjusting the garter on my thigh. "Give it a four-column spread on the society page and I'll guarantee a raise."

"Where, on the back of my skull? Get smart, Honey, you're the one who's playing with dynamite."

"Sure," I retorted. "I've got a stick of it up in my office right now. You want to light him?"

"He's already lit," Fred countered. "So's the rest of that Tunny gang. Adam Jason's the prime minister in charge of colonic baths, or didn't he try you for size?"

"Fred, I don't appreciate your brand of humor," I said tartly.

"And I don't appreciate your caliber of clients. I heard all that jazz in there."

"You're a good man with keyholes. It's a wonder your ears aren't shaped like a couple. You'd make a good second-story man on the ground floor."

He scowled. "Is that supposed to mean you weren't giving him the straight stuff in there?"

"You figure it out."

"All right," he said, his cane bracing him on the steps. "A guy winds up on a dirty asphalt road. A lady private eye bites some asphalt herself. The question is: Who's deadlier, the hairy men or the hairy spiders?"

I smiled thinly. "Hairy reporters with long canes are in a special category all their own. What do you know about Rip Spensor that's so deadly?"

"He worked for Tunny."

"Sure, and fought his way out. He was a decent guy, Fred."

"You'll have to prove it to me."

"Okay," I said. "I'm going up to Meadow Falls tomorrow with Adam. You want to tag along?"

"Not if I have to remove my clothes." He managed a half-grin.

"I can't guarantee anything. You'll have to stand up for yourself."

"I'm not much of a stand-up guy any more," he admitted.

"You make yourself sound like a coward, not a Medal of Honor winner."

He grimaced. "That hurt, Honey."

"I meant it to hurt," I said.

"Okay." He shrugged. "I'll go to Meadow Falls with you."

"Good," I said. "Meet me here in the alley at eleven. Adam has his own car. We'll follow."

He cocked his hat back with his cane. "I'll be here. Don't take any wooden tarantulas between now and then."

"This time I locked my car," I said. "Goodnight, Fred."

"Goodnight, Honey." He disappeared in the alley. I closed the back stairway door and moved toward my convertible. The fog had lifted now and stars gleamed in a cloudless dark sky. It would be dawn soon. I unlocked my car and stepped inside, eyes grazing over the seats and floor. There were no tarantulas.

But that was the least of my worries. Before I could close the door a figure moved into the opening and pressed a gun against my head. The figure was nude, dark-haired and voluptuous.

"This is where I came in," I said.

"This is where you go out," she corrected. "Start praying!"

FOUR

My arm lifted in the shallow light, chopping down hard on the slim, sun-tanned hand that clutched the gun. The heavy-handled instrument spun out of her grasp, thudding on the pavement. She bent to pick it up, but my other arm went around her throat. A scream twisted up in her throat, choked, and died as I threw her onto the seat beside me. She fell sideways against the steering wheel.

I flicked on my dash light and peered at her face.

"Angela Scali!" I said, as the glow illuminated her sensuous features.

"You filthy woman," the actress managed, with a trace of accent. "You killed my man."

"If you're talking about Rip Spensor," I said, "I don't own a steam roller."

She sat up, running slim fingers through long dark hair, teeth clenched. "You could have operated one," she said viciously. "I've heard about you. You're deadly."

"And you're naked. So what does that make you?"

"I'm a Sun Soul," she snapped. "We are the saviors of mankind."

I laughed. "The only thing you're saving, sister, is a fat clothing bill." I pushed her against the seat as she tried to squirm loose. "Now wise up or I'm going to have you clapped in a cell."

She had startling features. Deep brown eyes and a cleft in her chin. High cheekbones framed a delicately chiseled nose. Her lips were soft and full, like petals on a dew moistened rose.

"All right. I could be wrong," she said, rubbing her throat. "I—I'm sorry."

"You ought to be sorry," I said. "You've been living in rotten company. Do you realize that?"

Her eyes flashed. "No! Mr. Tunny and his directors are fine people. Not like those insane men in Hollywood. First you must sleep with them. Then you play the part. Italy was not like that."

I got out of the car and scooped up her gun. It was a German Luger. "Did you pick this up in Italy?"

"No. It belongs to Mr. Tunny's daughter, Toy. I stole it from her room."

I grinned. "She must be a cute Toy to fool around with this sort of plaything. I suppose that's all part of the religion."

Angela climbed from the car and stood beside me. She was a tall, graceful woman, and well-built. Obviously Italy's plentiful post-war years had been good to her.

"Mr. Tunny teaches peace," she said.

"I'll bet he does." I shoved her back inside the car.

"Come on, we're going to my apartment. I'm outfitting you in some clothes."

"No!" Her eyes flickered angrily.

"Don't argue with me," I said, sliding in beside her. "I'm trying to solve Rip Spensor's murder, but I can't do it with you running around like Lady Godiva without a horse."

Fortunately the fog deepened again out near Alamitos Bay. Several big trucks passed us on our way out of town and their drivers nearly went off the road after snatching a glimpse of Angela in their headlights.

I parked at the end of the street, below my second-story apartment, and got a blanket for the Italian Angel. She wrapped her abundant shape into the folds and followed me up the steps. I was careful not to forget her gun. It was a powerful weapon for a woman to be carrying.

I fixed us both a cup of coffee, lit the gas logs in my fireplace and joined her on the couch. She seemed dazed now, as if she'd been in some sort of shock and was just coming out of it. She peered about the living room stolidly, shaking her head.

"You seem confused," I offered.

"I—I am."

"How'd you travel from Meadow Falls to Long Beach?"

She brushed at her eyes. "What?"

"Now let's not play games, Miss Scali. This gun is no joke."

Her head jerked awkwardly. "What gun?"

I held up the Luger. "You said you stole this from Tunny's daughter, isn't that correct?"

Her tongue flicked wetly at the pale corners of her mouth. "I—I don't know what you're talking about."

I snapped my fingers several times in her face. She blinked and threw up her hands.

"What's the matter with you?" I demanded.

"I—I don't want any interviews now."

I straightened. "I'm no reporter."

"But—I just won an Academy Award."

"What?"

"An Academy Award," she said dazedly. "For the Best Actress of the Year."

"That was seven months ago, Miss Scali."

She got up, spilling her coffee. "You—you're lying."

"I wish I were. Sit down!"

"I can't!" she protested. "My agent, Sol Wetzel, he—he's waiting for me. We're going to a big celebration in honor of my Oscar."

I remembered reading about Angela Scali's disappearance. The night of the awards at the Pantages Theatre, she had accepted her Oscar, stepped out a side door to avoid photographers, and literally vanished into thin air.

"Miss Scali, either somebody has been drugging you or you've had amnesia. One way or the other, you seem to have dropped seven months out of your life."

She stared down at the blanket around her, then opened the folds and examined her bronzed naked body. "What's happened to my clothes?"

"Ask a guy named Thor Tunny," I said. "The saviour of mankind. He's apparently had you under lock and key for some time."

Tears sprang into her dark eyes. "But, I don't understand. I was at the Pantages Theatre in Hollywood. How—how did I get here?"

"That's a good question," I said. "Are you acquainted with a football player named Rip Spensor?"

"Yes. Rip and I date frequently. I plan to marry him."

"He's dead, Miss Scali!"

Her face crumpled. "No!"

"You accused me of murdering him," I said. "You came after me with this gun."

"I—I couldn't have. Why would I do that?"

I studied her carefully. It was possible she was lying. This could be a pretense. Another Academy Award performance. It was her eyes that made me think differently. But, then, I'd seen some of her pictures. She was a dedicated actress. Her eyes had a way of telling all sorts of lies.

"Adam Jason and Thor Tunny," I said. "Do they mean anything to you, Miss Scali?"

"The—the names do sound familiar."

"Meadow Falls?"

She shook her head dismally, rubbing her forehead. "Some—somehow," she stammered brokenly, her Italian accent suddenly more predominant than it had been before. "But—I can't imagine—"

I crossed to the telephone and dialed my office. It was time for a showdown. Adam had said he wasn't acquainted with Angela Scali. One of them was lying, and I had a hunch which one. The bell grated several times, then Charley April cut in. He was so tired he could hardly talk.

"Let the phone ring, Charley," I said. "There should be somebody in my office."

"Whatta you got," he blurted, "a party going on, Springtime?"

"Maybe."

"What happened to you out by the Anaheim bridge?"

"That's what I'd like to know."

The phone rang ten more times, then Charley said, "They've taken off, Honey."

"You don't know how right you are, Charley."

I hung up and stared at the Italian Angel. She stood before the fireplace, hands clutching the blanket, eyes wide.

"I've got a hunch we're in trouble," I said. "Real trouble. Do you know how to use this gun?"

She nodded hesitantly.

"Okay. I'm trusting you. I shouldn't, but—" I tossed her the Luger. "We may have a visitor before daylight."

"I—I don't understand," she said, staring at the gun.

"Neither do I, exactly. You disappeared mysteriously last March. You've apparently been living in the midst of a nude religious cult that quarters somewhere in the San Bernardino mountains. Rip Spensor has been linked with the group."

I took my revolver from its garter holster and laid it on the bar next to the telephone.

"I still don't understand," she said, frightened.

"You will if we get a visitor. I've got a hunch you escaped from Meadow Falls. They must have known you were going to come to me. That's why they sent Adam Jason."

She leaned against the fireplace and groaned. "Who are these people?"

"A frustrated group of fanatics," I said. "Living in a lost primeval world. Have you ever heard of the Penetantes?"

"No."

"Up until nineteen-thirty-six, they lived in the mountains of New Mexico. Their religious ceremonies involved stripping the young women naked and whipping them with lashes as they carried huge crosses on their backs."

She winced. "How awful."

"Thor Tunny has a new twist to the old theme. He conscripts beautiful young girls and uses them for what he will, religious purposes or not."

"But that's slavery."

"You're darned right," I said. "Proving it is another matter. Tunny claims he's running a legitimate nudist camp, based on a new Evangelistic doctrine. You're the first break we've had."

"We?"

"I'm a private detective," I said, letting my eyes shift toward the back door. "I work with the police and Sheriff's offices when I can. This adds up to one of those times."

Suddenly the lights went out. I reared up in the darkness, grasping my gun.

"What is it?" she demanded.

"Steady," I cautioned. "Somebody must have closed off the circuit breakers down in the garage. Keep that gun handy. The doors are locked, but they may try anything."

I picked up the phone and dialed the operator. "Give me the Sheriff's office," I said. In an instant I was connected to Homicide and Mark Storm.

"Marcus," I said quickly, "I'm at Alamitos Bay with Angela Scali. Somebody just cut off our electricity. They're after the Angel. Can you come out?"

"Don't kid me, Honey."

"I'm serious, Mark."

Footsteps fell harshly on the back staircase. Angela gasped.

Mark said angrily, "First it was tarantulas, then a naked man near the Anaheim bridge. What do you take me for?"

"I'll take you for a big boob if you don't get out here," I said, listening intently to the sounds at the rear of my apartment. The footsteps drew nearer, slamming heavily on the wet boards.

The deputy laughed. "And did Angela Scali present you with an Academy Award for this performance?"

"I'm not kidding, Lieutenant. She's here. Do you want to talk to her?"

"Sure," he said sarcastically. "Tell her it's Clark Gable. She'll know who I am."

The back door rattled violently.

"Mark," I said tersely. "There's going to be some shooting here in about five seconds. There's somebody at the kitchen door."

"It's the milkman, silly. Let him in. Show him your four-poster. He'll be interested."

The door smashed open from a vicious kick. I dropped the receiver and aimed my revolver toward the dark space that creaked open. Fog still drifted outside and I could smell its chill odor.

Then a high-pitched voice cried, "Angel!"

"Don't move," I whispered, not looking around at the Italian-born actress. "Don't move!"

I felt Angela's hand on mine. But that's not all I felt. Suddenly something crashed against the side of my head and I dropped. Off in a great distance, I heard stomping and smacking, but the noise was soon lost in the cool comfort of the hole I found myself falling into.

FIVE

"Honey!"

"Come on in. The water's fine."

"Honey!"

The other voice sounded a million miles away. Perched on a rock out in the middle of nowhere. Yelling at me like an infernal idiot.

"Put on your suit," I insisted, "and come on in!"

"My suit's on," the voice said. "You come out."

"I'm tired," I said. "Let me rest for a while, then I'll come out."

"You've been resting," the voice returned. "Four hours. Do you hear me?"

"I'm not deaf," I said, opening my eyes. Beyond was a fibrous pattern of arms, legs, and faces. I shook my head. "Is that you, Mark?"

"Yes!"

"What kept you?"

He groaned deeply. "A light on Seventh street. Are you awake?"

I laughed. "Set me up with five more of the same. Then leave the bottle."

"They left the bottle," Mark said distantly, "in your skull. Wake up, Honey!"

Mark slid into focus. His battered felt hat, his grim unshaven face, his slightly bent nose, his angry mouth.

I tried to sit up, but my head felt as if it were nailed to the floor.

"Who hit me?"

"From the looks of the lump I'd say three men and a horse. What happened?"

Sunlight streamed through a window above Mark's hunched shoulders. Another deputy stood next to the broad-shouldered lieutenant. Behind them was my back door, still ajar, wood splintered around the lock.

"Angela Scali pulled a sweet double-cross," I said, holding my head. "When my back was turned she clubbed me with a piece of German artillery."

"Then you weren't kidding about the Italian Angel being here?"

"Of course not." He lifted me to my feet. "That's what I get for being charitable. I hand out free blankets, free clothes and wind up with a two-story hangover. Remind me never to join the Salvation Army."

Fred Sims was perched on a bar stool in the kitchen, munching on a stale piece of bread. His eyes were haggard and deeply lined, and the scent of cheap whiskey floated up when he spoke.

"I warned you, Honey," the newsman said. "These people play for keeps. You're lucky."

"Yeah, lucky I don't have two heads."

Mark cocked his hat back and chewed on a fingernail sullenly. "Fred tells me you're working for Tunny."

I laughed. "If I am, he's got me digging my own grave."

"What are you going to do about it?" the deputy demanded.

I crossed into the kitchen, staggering a little and poured myself a cup of lukewarm coffee. "I'm going to pay Mr. Tunny a visit and return his compliment."

"I wouldn't do that if I were you."

"Lieutenant, if you were me you'd be knocking at his door right now with a steam roller in one hand and a basket of tarantulas in the other."

"You're wrong, Honey. Tunny's clean. I checked him out last night through the San Berdoo office. He was playing Scrabble about the time you and Spensor bit the asphalt."

"Who says?"

"He's got a dozen different witnesses."

"Sure," I said. "One who's an expert at operating a steam roller and another who runs a tarantula farm. Wake up, Lieutenant, he's got these people drugged."

"What do you mean?"

"Either that or he has them hypnotized," I sipped at my coffee. "You should have seen Angela Scali. She was way out in left field before I brought her here. It could have been an act, but I don't think so. She suddenly started making sense."

"Then why'd she slug you?"

I shook my head. "I don't know. Someone called her name. It was weird, like an echo drifting down from a mountain. It must have affected her somehow."

"Honey, that doesn't make sense," the big deputy barked.

"It does if she was responding to a post-hypnotic suggestion," I said. "Her name pitched in a certain way might have been all that was needed to put her under again."

"Maybe, but I don't buy witchcraft."

I shrugged. "Then you explain Angela Scali's disappearance. But don't waste Fred's time—or mine—with your explanation because we're on our way to Meadow Falls."

Fred stiffened. "Not me."

"You kidding?" I said. "It'll be the story of a lifetime."

"That's what I'm afraid of," Fred answered, rapping his cane on the bar. "I'm planning to live to be a hundred. There are more stories to write than Tunny's. Like your obituary."

I patted him on the head. "Brave warrior. Heap big courage. Just don't trip on your own scalp."

"Fred makes sense, Honey," Mark argued. "You'd better stay away from Meadow Falls and Thor Tunny."

"You said he was harmless, Lieutenant. He's probably a nice old guy with false teeth and a cellar full of bodies."

"I told you Tunny's clean."

"What is this, Lieutenant, Dodge Honey Day? With a steam roller murder on your hands, I'm sure you're not just going to sit around your office and cut out paper dolls."

His forehead ridged angrily. "I'd like to cut you out, Honey. And plaster you on my wall."

I grinned. "Come now, Lieutenant, you must have a better place in mind to put me."

Fred chuckled. "Marcus, she's got you again."

The crippled reporter tucked the remainder of the bread in his mouth and took my hand. "Let's go."

"But you said—"

"I said the same thing at Bastogne," he blared. "The only trouble was I didn't have a compass. Instead of winding up at the rear lines, I walked into a German machine-gun nest. It was damned embarrassing."

I patted his cheek tenderly. "Okay, Private Sims, let's be embarrassed together. We've done it before."

"You can say that again, Miss West. I'll never forget Las Vegas."

"And neither will I." I gestured as if I was tipping my hat at Mark Storm. "See you, Lieutenant. Come visit us sometime for a game of Scrabble."

"You idiots," the deputy said, throwing up his arms. "You'll wind up with two canes and a tin cup. Don't fool with Tunny."

"You told us he was clean," I said. "We'll send you a report. Bye."

Fred and I waltzed out arm in arm. The sun was hot for an October morning. At Meadow Falls it would be much warmer. That we knew.

The drive in my convertible took a little over two hours. Rain was falling in Lake Arrowhead when we passed, and the mountains were bright green and shiny. By the time we reached Meadow Falls, the clouds had vanished and the sun glared brilliantly on the tents and buildings belonging to Tunny's nude health cult.

We were met at the gate by a big man with a hairy chest and a visored cap. He had more muscle than a gorilla and about as much brain.

"What do you want?" he demanded.

"We're putting ourselves through college," I said. "Wouldn't you like to buy a subscription?"

"No!" he bellowed, scratching his thick, completely-shaven head. "This is the Holy Sanctuary of the Sun Souls. Go away or take off your clothes!"

I nudged the ponderous gatekeeper and winked. "How about a partial membership? We'll take off some of our clothes."

The gatekeeper lifted his visor and examined me carefully. "You'd have to speak with Mr. Tunny first. We don't allow peddlers on the grounds."

"Even if they are selling sun oil?" I removed a bottle of suntan lotion from my glove compartment. "Friend, I ask you, aren't you burning in places you wish you weren't?"

His fleshy face reddened. "Well, I—"

"See what I mean," I said. "Your flock is just itching to be annointed by our holy oil. Now be a good boy and let us through."

"No!" he roared. "This is the morning of the Special Council. All that are holy have convened in the temple to hear Mr. Tunny speak of peace."

I glanced at Fred. "Tunny has a one-track soul. Mr. Sims, don't you think we should at least endow this holy member with our ointment before leaving these hallowed grounds?"

Fred removed the bottle from my hands. "By all means, Miss West. Allow me."

The newspaperman stepped from the car, pushing himself forward with the aid of his cane. He had a determined look on his face, but he seemed to be enjoying this. The hairy-chested gatekeeper moved around in front of Fred, flexing his powerful arms.

"So it's you again, huh?" the gatekeeper said. "Didn't I warn you earlier to stay away?"

"I don't know what you're talking about." The reporter removed the cap from the bottle and shook it vigorously. "Smell this," he said. "Have you ever inhaled nectar of the gods?"

"There is only one god," the gatekeeper said. "And he is the god of all flesh."

"That's what I mean," Fred replied, moving nearer to the other man.

Suddenly the contents gushed in the gatekeeper's face. He staggered back, trying to wipe his eyes. Fred's cane whirled, cracking against his knuckles, then against his bronzed skull. The naked man crumpled soundlessly in the dirt, unconscious.

Before I could start the engine, Fred was in the car beside me.

"Okay, Miss West," he said, eyes glowing weirdly. "He's been annointed. Let's go."

"Sims, you haven't lost your touch," I said.

He glanced down at his crippled leg and at his cane. "What I've lost in flesh, I've gained in hickory. Who can say my loss is not our gain."

"I'm with you," I said, shifting into low. The convertible shot forward toward the holy grounds of the Sun Souls. "By the way, what did he mean about warning you earlier?"

Fred stared at the windshield grimly. "Darned if I know."

We parked in front of the temple and climbed out into blazing mid-day sunshine. Tunny's huge building was amazingly modern. It was constructed of glass and brick and on the front was a colorful mosaic of a naked woman lying on a bed of roses. From where we stood we could hear the sound of a man's voice blaring angrily inside the temple. He was condemning something or someone in a vicious, snarling way that was half whimper, half shout. We walked up the steps, Fred's cane thudding on the brick, and into a multi-colored hall where a group of nude men and women knelt, their backs turned toward us.

High on a rostrum, beyond a pane of glass, stood an immense man with flame-red hair and glowering eyes. Even from this distance it was obvious he was at least seven feet tall.

"Holy smokes," Fred whispered. "A redheaded King Kong."

Behind Tunny was the statue of a naked man and

woman entwined around a tree of snakes, arms lifted frantically.

The huge man struck the speaker's stand with his fist. "Fools! Is there not one of you who can explain the disappearance of our princess? Is there not one of you who saw her leave the camp?" His face and powerful body were darkly tanned. "If she is not returned the heavens will rage down upon us. The seas will rise and flood the land. The mountains will quake and the trees will burn."

"He must be talking about Angela Scali," I whispered.

"But I thought you said they took her from your apartment."

"I don't know who took her," I said. "Don't put words in my mouth."

Fortunately, none of Tunny's disciples looked around. They kept their heads bowed, nude backs bent, bottoms resting on their heels. At least a hundred of them knelt humbly before the candle-lit dais.

"Someone must have helped her escape," Tunny continued, throwing a piercing gaze on the gathering. "If this be true, this person shall live in fear and trembling, and from this day forward shall walk upon the face of this earth with a terrible weight on his back."

Suddenly he saw us through the glass screen and his eyes widened.

"The jig's up," I said. "Now don't panic. Just keep smiling as if you'd wandered into the wrong rest room during a coffee break."

"Who are these intruders?" Tunny demanded.

The congregation turned, squinting at Fred and me, a panorama of bare chests, dazed faces and open mouths.

I moved into the aisle, grasping Fred's hand and said, "Excuse the interruption, but we were wondering if you could tell us the way to the County Fair. You see, we made a wrong turn about a thousand miles back—"

"Heathens!" Tunny roared. "How dare you wear garments into our sacred temple!"

Adam Jason popped from behind an ornate screen and waved his arms. "Wait a minute, Mr. Tunny. That's Honey West, the female investigator."

Tunny's scowl vanished. He moved to the edge of the rostrum. "The congregation is dismissed," he said. "Return to your separate quarters and remain there until further notice."

The Sun Souls began to file out quietly, threading around Fred and me like they were in some sort of trance. They resembled naked zombies, eyes staring in their sunburnt heads, legs moving mechanically, lips taut in their faces. Most of them were young, about my age, and handsome.

When they were gone, Tunny came down from the speaker's platform slowly, his huge body towering in the aisle.

"Well, Miss West, it appears you have accepted our offer," he said. "Welcome to Meadow Falls."

"I've accepted nothing, Mr. Tunny. I'm here because of an incident which occurred in my apartment early this morning. Where's Angela Scali?"

Tunny's red-rimmed eyes quickly shifted to Adam and back to me. Close up, he was an extraordinary looking man. His flaming hair was obviously dyed. So were his eyebrows. He had a cruel, hard mouth and a red-veined nose that was flattened at the end as if it had been brutally beaten at one time. He seemed like some awesome, gigantic devil, half-smiling, half-glowering, fists balled on his naked hips, legs apart.

"I don't understand, Miss West," he said, glancing at Fred. "Angela who?"

"Scali. The Italian Angel. Winner of this year's Academy Award. Don't be coy, Mr. Tunny."

He scratched at his ear thoughtfully. "I'm afraid you have me, Miss West. We here at Meadow Falls frown highly on the quixotic medium of the motion picture. Perhaps Adam has heard of this wonderous woman, but not I."

Adam brushed at his hairy chest, trying to avoid my burning stare. "We don't sanction movies, Honey."

"What do you sanction?" I demanded, looking beyond at the naked replica of two humans welded together by twisting snakes. "Who's your missing princess?"

"She is sacred," Tunny said abruptly. "A flower born not of this Earth. She has no name. Only a fragrance. A fragrance of the hills and the valleys and the snow-capped peaks. She is immortal."

Tunny wore a bronze medallion about his neck, suspended on a thin chain. He began to tap the shiny piece with the tip of his finger nervously. I guessed he was in his mid-fifties. Maybe less. He had deep crow's feet at the outer edge of each eye, curving down onto his cheeks.

"Miss West, we were hoping you'd help us," Tunny said irritatedly, after a moment. "You're a lovely woman. So blonde and fair. So richly vibrant. You are a princess, also. But you have arsenic in your veins."

"That's funny," I said. "Last night a medical examiner called it tarantula poison."

Tunny grasped his medallion with both hands. "I sense spiritual interference here. You may go, Miss West. We will forward a check to you for your trouble. Now our association is terminated."

"Not by a long shot," I said, yawning suddenly.

Tunny's medallion trembled in his fingers. I couldn't seem to take my eyes off it. A relaxed feeling surged through me. Like a velvet hand stroking my back, soothing my aching head. The bronze disk kept flicking, glittering harshly in the temple's dim light.

"You're tired, Miss West," Tunny said softly, eyes piercing into me. "Very sleepy."

I nodded. "You—you're so right. I only got an hour or so this morning. And that was through the courtesy of an Adolph Hitler gun factory."

"Both of you," Tunny continued, fixing his gaze on Fred. "Relax all your muscles. You are going into a deep sleep. Deeper and deeper. You are falling asleep. Deeper and deeper."

The medallion twitched and glittered in his fingers.

Fred sagged slowly to the floor, curling an arm under his head, eyes closed.

Tunny's gaze shifted back to me. "You feel warm in all those clothes, my lovely princess. Remove your sweater and relax. You are sleeping, but your eyes shall remain open."

I stretched. "It—it is hot in here."

"Remove your sweater!"

I found myself slipping the garment over my head. The medallion seemed to glow now, burning away the temple and the two naked men and Fred lying on the floor. I stepped out of my skirt.

"That's much better," I heard my voice say. It seemed so distant I could barely recognize it as my own. Suddenly I felt as if I were on fire. I squirmed uncomfortably. Then kicked off my shoes.

"You're doing well, princess," Tunny's voice soothed. "The snaps are at the back. Undo them! Don't confine yourself. Relax. Feel free. Feel the air and the coolness of the mountains on your body. Deliver all your sins up to heaven. Stand straight and tall in this sanctified temple. Be as you were when you were born."

The medallion rolled in his huge fingers, flicking light in my eyes, soothing me, relaxing me with each new twist.

"You are the princess of all you survey," the voice droned. "You are beautiful. Remove the last remnants of your past life and step forth free upon this land that is yours to rule."

The medallion twisted back and forth, back and forth. Suddenly something jammed against it hard. Tunny fell back from the impact. I shook my head. Fred

Sims stood before the massive naked man, his cane lodged against Tunny's chest.

"You dirty bastard!" Fred growled. "I'm going to poke this stick right through you!"

"But—but you were asleep," Tunny stammered.

"You thought I was asleep," Fred blared. "That's where you made your mistake." He snapped his fingers several times. "Wake up, Honey. Put your clothes on."

"What?"

I glanced down. My clothing was strewn around the floor. I lifted my arms to my chest. "He hypnotized us," I said.

"He tried," Fred countered, snatching the medallion from Tunny's chest. "Two more seconds and you would have been downright naked."

Adam Jason grabbed Fred's cane and hurled him backward, but I stopped the reporter before he fell. I leveled my revolver and said, "You never should have done that, Adam. I liked you up until now. This cuts it."

"You don't understand, Honey," Adam said. "Mr. Tunny was trying to help you."

"Sure, help me into a pine box." I held the gun on the two men. "Where's Angela Scali?"

"We—we don't know," Adam returned.

"Then you do admit the Italian Angel is your sacred princess?"

"Yes," Tunny said, biting his lips. "But we have no idea what happened to Angela. She vanished last night. I sent Adam out looking for her."

"And he found her," I said, trying to cover myself

with my free hand. "He kicked in my kitchen door and hauled her out by the hair, didn't you. Adam?"

"No!"

"I suppose you didn't leave my office, either."

"I had to, Honey. I walked back to that bridge, got my car and returned to Meadow Falls."

"Why?"

"I couldn't find Angela. I had to report to Mr. Tunny."

"You're lying, Adam. Somehow Angela's mixed up with Rip Spensor's murder, isn't she? You and Tunny knew that. That's why you went after her."

Adam straightened angrily. "No, Honey. You've got this all wrong."

"She was under a hypnotic spell," I said. "She confessed rationally that she knew nothing about Meadow Falls."

"She was lying," Tunny broke. "Angela came here under her own power. She pleaded with me to take her into the organization. To keep her name anonymous."

"You can do better than that," I said.

Adam's eyes narrowed, flicking for an instant at Fred. "Mr. Tunny's telling you the truth, Honey. Both Angela Scali and Rip Spensor were unhappy people. We tried to help them."

"Sure you did. The same way you tried to help me a few minutes ago. Have you got the whole congregation in a hypnotic trance?"

Thor Tunny staggered slightly. "Don't be ridiculous!"

Suddenly Mark Storm burst through the temple doors. He had several other deputies with him and, from the looks on their faces, I could tell something terrible had happened. The lieutenant's mouth was twisted angrily and his tie hung in two gnarled ribbons down the front of his shirt.

He swore when he saw me. "Honey, I should have known you'd go native. Get your clothes on!"

"What are you doing here, Lieutenant? You said Tunny was clean."

"He's clean, all right," Mark blared. "We've found the Italian Angel."

"Where?"

"Hanging from a tree, down near the falls. She's about as clean as he is. There's blood all over her."

SIX

High along the mountain a ribbon of water tumbled crazily over a rocky slope, slithered through brush and low-hanging trees, finally pitching itself into a small stream that cut back of Tunny's camp. Angela Scali dangled, a thick cord knotted around her throat, from a branch above the stream. The rush of water splattered on her slim legs, dripping off onto a mossy bank that was red from Angela's blood.

She twisted and swayed in the breeze, arms hanging at her sides, hair swirling about her bronzed face. At times the branch would drop her to within arm's reach of someone standing on the mossy bank, then a gust of wind would thrust her skyward, legs jerking like a toy doll, blood oozing from the many wounds. Her killer had done a thorough job. She had been knifed at least a dozen times in the abdomen and chest.

After cutting the body down, Mark joined me at the top of a ravine. Sweat streamed from beneath his hat and he wiped at it clumsily with a handkerchief.

"This is as bad as the steam roller," he said.

I grimaced, staring around at the mute, dead-eyed Sun Souls who stood on the hillside above the stream. "Who found her?"

"We don't know. I was at the San Berdoo office when an anonymous tip came in. We couldn't trace it."

"Man or woman?"

"Too muffled to tell." He groaned. "Is this going to make headlines! Fred nearly went berserk."

Wind ruffled my hair. "So I noticed. He cried, he was so excited. You've got blood on your suit."

Mark dabbed at some dark spots on his coat. "You can imagine what her murderer looked like after he strung her up. I've never seen so much blood."

I walked to the edge of the ravine and watched them photograph Angela and wrap her in a rubber sheet. It reminded me of a scene from one of her movies, but I knew she couldn't step out of the sheet and walk away if the director shouted, "Cut!" They carried her to an ambulance parked near the mountain stream. Her dark hair trailed down from one corner of the sheet.

Mark came up behind me and said, "We must be dealing with a maniac. He made a pin cushion out of her. She was probably dead long before he hung her up."

I nodded. "If he's a nudist you're not going to find any blood-stained clothes, unless he wore shoes."

"No indications down there whether he did or didn't. Too much moss along the bank."

Thor Tunny joined us, stroking his thick red-dyed

hair. "I'm sorry. This is extremely gruesome."

My head snapped around, eyes flashing. "Angela Scali's dead, Mr. Tunny. Maybe I would have wound up in the same rubber sheet if Fred hadn't stayed awake."

"My dear Miss West," he protested, "my hypnotic trance was only an act. It was not meant to injure you in any way."

"You got me out of my clothes, Mr. Tunny," I said. "What were you trying for, bingo?"

Even Mark Storm seemed dwarfed beside the towering hulk of the nude cult leader. The deputy swung around in front of the other man and said, "Tunny, you're in serious trouble. You realize that, don't you?"

"A murder on my property is serious," Tunny said. "I refuse to admit anything else, though, until I converse with my lawyer."

"What about this hypnotic trance business?" Mark demanded.

"Well?"

"Do you keep your members under a spell?"

A sarcastic smile spread on Tunny's mouth. "Don't be asinine. We use hypnosis in some of our teachings. That's all."

"Don't let him con you, Mark," I said. "These people make Barney Google look sick. They walk around like zombies."

Tunny laughed. "Miss West, you are obviously the victim of too many late late movies. You're free to question any of my congregation. That light you see in their eyes is the light of love and tranquility."

"I'll bet," I said. "Do you have a daughter named Toy?"

"Yes."

"Where is she?"

"I have no idea," Tunny answered. "She doesn't follow our doctrines too closely. Once a week she goes into town."

"Without clothes?"

"Of course not!"

Sunlight seared our faces, burning across the green hills, reflected off the quiet stream and tumbling waterfall. Beyond Tunny, high along a ridge where a fire trail swathed a dark path through the trees, I noticed a solitary cabin.

Shielding my eyes, I gestured toward the mountaintop. "Who lives up there?"

"No one," Tunny said. "It's been vacant for years. Used to house forest ranger equipment for fire fighting, but it was abandoned when we built here in Meadow Falls."

Dark clouds began to pile up behind the ridge, moving swiftly across the blue sky.

"Looks like we're in for a thunder storm," Mark said, examining the sky. "Come on, Tunny, deputies from the San Berdoo office want to ask you a few questions."

Just as they turned their backs something glinted in one of the cabin windows, as if a mirror had been held to catch the sun's rays. I blinked, then glanced at Mark. His gaze was on the cult leader as they started down toward the camp. The light flashed again. Someone was signaling!

"Hey, Lieutenant," I said.

"Later, Honey," Mark returned, not looking around.

They disappeared into a grove of trees, the deputy jogging behind Tunny, hat jammed low on his big head.

Thunder split hard above the mountains and the valley. The ambulance was gone now. So were the Sun Souls and the other deputies. I stood alone above the quiet stream, my eyes pinned on the cabin.

When a third flash came, I started up the side of the mountain. Luckily I'd worn flats. There was no trail to follow and I stumbled several times in thick brush. I kept glancing back toward camp in case someone tried to return the signal, but nothing glittered except the glass dome of Tunny's modern temple. During the arduous journey I tried to mesh together my thoughts on Angela Scali's death. She'd been taken from my apartment around five A.M. Sheriff's deputies found her body about noon. Seven hours. During that time somebody had kicked in my back door and spirited Angela to Meadow Falls. Then she had been lured to a spot near the falls where she was stabbed and hung. Had it been the same person in both instances? If so, why had he waited? Why didn't he murder her in my apartment? Why travel over a hundred miles to commit such a grisly crime? There must have been two people. One the intruder. The other the murderer. The first could have returned her safely to Meadow Falls, then left her. The second might have been waiting, enticed her to the mountain stream, and used the knife.

The sky darkened. Thunder rumbled again, breaking over the mountains in fitful angry spasms. Rain began to pelt down and wind rose up from the valley below, blowing hair in my eyes, lifting my skirt.

Finally, I reached a grove of trees about fifty yards from the cabin. Huge drops slashed between branches, drenching me to the skin. I suddenly realized I was taking a desperate chance. Angela's killer might have climbed the mountain and secreted himself in the cabin. The signal puzzled me, though. Who could have been waiting for it, and why?

I removed my .22 revolver and crept toward the cabin slowly in the gathering darkness. The journey up the mountain had taken more than an hour and my legs ached, my heart pounded. The rain fell heavily on the trees and the mountaintop and the dark cabin. Wind whistled fiercely over the ridge. Thunder jolted.

The cabin was larger than it had appeared from below. A shutter on one of the windows banged. So did the front door. I approached cautiously in a half-crouch, gun leveled.

A few feet from the door I flattened against a wall and tried to catch my breath. A trail led away from the cabin down the other side of the mountaintop. It was possible that whoever signaled had already left via that path. The drenching rain made me think otherwise. The cabin was at least a shelter until the downpour ceased. I was soaked and trembling as I crept nearer. The door banged back and forth in the wind.

I timed the door's swing, shielding my eyes. It swung out, wavered and then thudded back loudly. I planned to stop it as it wavered, step inside and catch the signaler off-guard.

The door banged again. Opened and wavered. I stepped forward into the opening, but suddenly its pattern changed. The panel closed against me. Hard, I nearly lost my revolver, stumbled and fell inside the cabin as the door's weight jammed against me.

"Is that you, Toy?" a voice demanded.

I straightened, pushing myself up, trying to distinguish shapes inside the shadowed cabin. I saw an old table and a chair, two or three boxes stacked in one corner. Rain beat against a single window on the far side. In front of this was the outline of a man, standing, his shoulders hunched.

"Don't move," I said. "I've got a gun."

"What?"

Water streamed down from my wet hair, half-blinding me. "Turn toward the window, hands above your head, legs apart."

He whirled, framed in the faded light of the window, and lifted his arms. "I—I don't get this," he stammered. "You're a woman, aren't you?"

"So I've been told. Palms flat on the wall! Quickly!"

He followed my orders, head slouched between his shoulders, legs apart. He was well built and tall. That much I could see. He practically blotted out the window. I advanced slowly until my free hand was on his back.

"You're wet," he said.

"It's raining. Or didn't you notice."

"I didn't notice you coming up the mountain. What trail did you take?"

He wore a bright yellow letterman's sweater. I searched in the pockets. They were empty. His pants contained a wallet and a ring of keys.

"That tickles," he said, as I drew my hand out of one of the pockets.

"Turn around!" I directed curtly. "Slow."

Again he followed my instructions without hesitation. In the faint glare of the window I saw a grinning, broad mouth, a deep dimple in his right cheek, sandy blond hair that slanted carelessly on his forehead, intense brown eyes. He was somewhere in his twenties, husky, handsome and cocky as hell.

"Hey, you—you're pretty," he said, arms still raised. He had started to say something else, then changed his mind. I had a feeling he knew me. I ran my revolver snout against his shirt pockets. They, too, were empty.

Then I stepped back, wiping my face with the back of my hand. "Okay," I said. "Where's the knife?"

"What knife? You crazy or something?"

"No, but I'm looking for somebody who is. What's your name?"

"Spensor. Ray Spensor."

"Rip's cousin?"

"That's right. Who are you?"

"I think you already know."

He shook his head, eyes riveted on my soaking wet sweater. "Marilyn Monroe?"

"Don't be funny."

"From what I can see you look like her, except for the gun. May I lower my hands now?"

"No. What are you doing up here?"

"Waiting for a streetcar. What's your explanation?"

"Your signal," I said, brushing water from my hair. "I thought maybe you were in trouble. And I gather you are."

Wind and rain beat at the cabin furiously.

"I'm a mountain climber," he said, still grinning. "I mistook these for the Alps. My mistake."

"The only mistake you made was thinking I was Tunny's daughter. Where is she?"

"How should I know?"

"You called for Toy when I came in."

The grin spread wider on his handsome face. "I'm just a kid at heart. Can I help it if I lost my rocking horse when I was five?"

"You're going to lose more than that if you don't straighten up," I threatened.

"I'm as straight as I can get," he said mockingly. "Damn, you look good in a wet sweater."

"As good as the Italian Angel looked hanging from that tree?"

His thick brows lifted slightly. "What are you talking about?"

"Don't play dumb, pal, you saw the ambulance."

He glanced toward the window. "Is—is that what that was? I thought it was some sort of special celebration. Everybody was grouped around that tree. I—"

"Angela Scali's dead."

His head jerked, eyes widening. "I—I don't believe you!"

"Somebody carved her up like a Christmas turkey." My glare was acid.

"You—you don't think that I—?"

"You haven't explained why you're up here yet."

He nodded dismally. "I *am* waiting for Toy Tunny. She and I brought Angela back to the camp this morning."

My hand tightened harshly on the revolver. "So you're the guy who broke into my apartment?"

He paused, then, "Yes. I'm sorry. I—I didn't realize you'd be hurt."

"What'd you expect? An ice cream party?"

"Toy told me everything would be all right. When we got inside you were lying on the floor. Angela had a gun in her hands."

"She sure did," I said. "How do you figure in this?" He lowered his arms half-way, head shaking "Rip's my cousin. We played together for the Rams."

"That doesn't gain you much yardage with Angela Scali. You're hiding out in a cabin above the falls where she died. You've admitted breaking into my place to get her."

"I didn't want to leave you lying there, but what could I do?"

"You could have put a knife in my ribs."

He leaned back against the window. "I didn't touch you, or Angela. I brought her to the camp and left her outside her apartment. And that was the end of that."

"Far from it," I said. "You're here. On the mountain. You were signaling. Don't tell me that's how you get a streetcar in the rain."

"I—I," he stammered. "Toy told me to come up here."

"Why?"

"I don't know," he said flatly. "She's a peculiar person. She said she had some evidence that would point to Rip's killer."

A voice broke behind me. "And I wasn't kidding, baby."

I whirled. A naked woman with short brown hair stood framed in the doorway. She had a German Luger aimed at my head.

"Drop it, Miss West."

The revolver slipped from my fingers, clattering on the wood floor. "So we finally meet, Miss Tunny."

"You've been getting in our way, Miss West. I don't like that."

"Toy," Spensor broke, "she says Angela's dead."

"She is," Toy answered, flicking green eyes at the husky Rams football player. "Unfortunately she is, Ray. I'm sorry."

"You're sorry!" Spensor roared, moving around the table. "That's great. How did it happen?"

"Somebody was hiding in her apartment." Toy said, gesturing with the Luger. "Back up, Miss West. I know you're full of tricks. So we won't stand on formality. Okay?"

Toy Tunny was well named. She wasn't much larger than a doll. In the storm's muted light her round, wide eyes seemed as if they were made of glass. Her arms and legs were pudgy and dimpled. She was dripping wet from the rain and she brushed her hair as she leaned down for my revolver.

Ray Spensor crossed to the window again where rain still slashed heavily at the glass. "Toy, you shouldn't do this," he protested.

"Don't be silly, baby," she said, rubbing her round little stomach with the butt of my revolver. "It's either her or us. I heard what she said. She could hang a noose around our necks."

"But we didn't do anything," Spensor argued.

"These private dicks don't care about evidence, baby." She lifted the Luger into my face. "Strip down, Miss West."

"What?"

"I said take off your clothes. And be quick about it. You're going to spend some time up here. At least, until we can get away."

"Now look, Miss Tunny, I already went through this routine with your father and besides—"

Her finger tightened on the trigger. "She doesn't want to cooperate, baby. I guess you'll have to do the honors. It won't be the first time."

"Toy!" Spensor erupted.

"Do you want to hang for the Angel?" Toy demanded, harshly.

"Well, no, but—"

"Then get busy."

Spensor advanced toward me, an apologetic look on his handsome face. "Please, Honey."

"No *please* about it, baby," Toy blurted. "My car's parked on the South Mountain Road. Even with her stripped and tied we're going to be lucky if we get through the Sheriff's barricade below Arrowhead. I'll wear her skirt and sweater."

"They won't fit you, Toy," Spensor said, reaching around my waist.

Toy laughed, her pudgy frame shaking. "The cops shouldn't notice if the rain keeps up. I'll be hunched in the seat."

"You're making a mistake, Miss Tunny," I said, as Spensor peeled my wet sweater up over my bra. "If you're innocent I could help you."

"It isn't a question of innocence," Toy answered, rubbing at her freckled cheeks. "It's a question of guilt. Now with Angela dead, I know who the murderer is." Spensor ripped off my sweater and glowered at the other woman. "You talk too much, Toy."

"Just trying to be helpful, baby," she said, smiling. "Maybe Miss West means what she says. If that's true she ought to look up Sol Wetzel, Angela's agent."

"Why?" I demanded.

"Because he was in love with the Angel. Madly. He hated any rivals."

Spensor's fingers dug impatiently at the hooks on my brassiere, "Toy, that's enough!"

"Okay," she said, tossing him a length of rope from one of the boxes. "Get her skirt and let's blow this joint."

He jerked down on my skirt zipper and I stepped out slowly, trying to figure a way I could stop them from leaving me behind in the cabin. There seemed to be only one avenue, and that was through Ray Spensor. I whirled on him, crushing against his thick chest.

"Hey!" he blurted.

"I need you," I whispered in his ear. "Don't leave me!"

The storm was so loud outside the cabin I was sure Toy Tunny hadn't heard what I'd said. She pressed the gun against my spine hard.

"No nonsense, Miss West. Lover is a sensitive guy. You're liable to shake up his molecules. Down, girl."

I clung for an instant, my face buried in his neck. "Come back for me," I whispered, as a clap of thunder rattled the cabin. "You won't be sorry."

Spensor pushed me away from him, his eyes narrowed in the semi-darkness, mouth twisted.

I knew I'd made progress. His mouth opened over straight white teeth and he took a deep breath, eyes still fixed on me, a hungry, searching look that said, *"I want you!"*

"The rope, lover," Toy said. "She's only a woman. You've seen dozens of them in the Playground."

"I know," he said mechanically. "She—"

Toy placed both guns in his hands and grabbed the rope. She tied my hands behind my back, then pulled me to the floor.

"You'll thank me for this someday, Miss West," she said, looping the rope around my feet and knotting it harshly.

"Maybe I'll return the favor," I said. "Only mine'll be around your fat little neck."

Her eyes lighted angrily. "Don't be sour, lambie. Somebody'll rescue you before tomorrow. Maybe a forest ranger. They love coming up here and peeking down at the naked girlies."

"You don't go much for your father's religion, do you, Miss Tunny?" I said, writhing from the rope burns on my wrists.

"Are you kidding?" Toy wrinkled her freckly nose, taking Spensor's hand. "Dad is the original con man. He started in carnivals years ago. He was the ventriloquist, the mystic, the hypnotist. For money he'll do anything. Molest teen-age girls. Dance on graves. Watch out for him, Honey! He's no good."

"Toy!" Spensor protested again, glaring down at me.

"Come on, lover," the pudgy girl said, grabbing my clothes. "We've got a rendezvous with Sol Wetzel. See you in the funny papers, Honey."

She jerked Ray Spensor through the door. For an instant, I could hear them running across the fire break toward the path down the mountain, then a surge of thunder drowned their movements and rain began to pelt hard on the roof. I wriggled around for fully five minutes trying to reach the knots Toy had tied, but they were impossible. It got darker. And bitterly cold. Through the window above my head rain splattered in on my face, cooling my anger, but not helping my predicament.

I couldn't understand why Toy had tied me up. It didn't make sense unless she was involved in either Rip Spensor's death or Angela Scali's. I thought back to the night before when I'd found tarantulas in my car. This was the kind of country where spiders of that variety thrived. They lived in holes in the side of the hills.

The door banged, swung open and banged again. I was hoping Ray Spensor would come back. I didn't relish spending a night in this cabin. And then there was the possibility no one would find me even tomorrow. Thor Tunny had said this cabin had been abandoned by the forest rangers. If I couldn't escape the rope, I might be here for days, even weeks. Maybe that was what Toy had in mind.

Suddenly I heard footsteps outside.

"Hey!" I cried. "In here!"

They drew nearer, muted by the thunder and rain.

Then the door opened again and I saw the outline of a man standing there, a hat slouched on his head, his shoulders bent against the storm.

"Here!" I yelled loudly. "I'm tied on the floor! Help me!"

The figure moved forward slowly, his face hidden by the darkness. One leg dragging under him, a cane thudding on the wood floor.

"Fred?" I demanded. "Is that you?"

The man didn't answer. He moved around the table, cane clopping, leg dragging, head bent.

"Fred?" I repeated.

Thunder rolled harshly in the sky, shaking the cabin. He stood above me, a seemingly huge figure. His cane lifted.

"Honey?" The voice sounded like Fred's, but I wasn't certain.

"Here," I pleaded. "Here, Fred!"

The cane swung in an angry arc, thudding on my shoulder. I screamed from the pain.

"Fred!"

Thunder crashed wildly. So did the voice.

"I'm going to kill you, Honey!"

SEVEN

The cane smashed against my ribs.

"Fred!"

I spun forward, the rope tearing at my flesh, and crashed against the table. Wood splintered as it toppled over on the floor.

"Honey!" the figure cried, as he stepped around the broken piece of furniture, face hidden in the darkness.

His cane swung again, grazing my leg, bringing another cry from my lips. I rolled on my shoulder, kicking up my heels frantically, pushing myself toward the door. The wood surface burned my back and arms as I moved.

He came after me, his cane rattling on the floor. He brought it down again on my shoulder, the shaft cutting into my flesh.

I kicked at him. One ankle struck his right hip and he lost his balance. He fell hard, groaning from the impact.

Thunder rattled above the mountaintop.

Gritting my teeth for all I was worth, I shoved myself toward the door. I could manage to wriggle caterpillar-fashion. He got to his feet slowly, bracing himself with the cane, his shadow huge along the cabin's ceiling.

I reached the door and tumbled out into the rain and mud. He came after me, cane lifted again, leg dragging behind.

"Fred, you idiot, it's me!" I screamed.

The late afternoon sky was pitch black and failed to cast any light on the advancing man's face as he staggered out onto the ridge.

His cane flicked again, slamming down on my head. I kicked, reeled, my senses spinning from the blow, the sky turning wildly over me.

Suddenly I found myself on the crest of the mountain where the fire break slanted down to a grove of trees hundreds of feet below. I teetered on the edge, looked back at the advancing figure, and pitched myself over.

The first few yards were easy. Then it seemed as if the rope was tearing me to pieces. I screamed. Blackness came up and smacked me in the face and I stopped screaming and just relaxed. I felt mud in my mouth and rain drilling on my flesh. And suddenly I wasn't rolling any more. And even with the rain and thunder I could hear the steady crunch crunch of someone coming down the mountain after me.

"My God, you're lucky," a voice said. "You could have been killed."

I felt strong arms under me and I writhed, anticipating more blows from a cane.

I opened my eyes. Ray Spensor's handsome face loomed over me, mouth taut. Beyond I saw the cabin's worn wood beams. He carried me into it and set me down gently.

"You—you came back," I stammered.

"Of course, I did," he said, bending over me. "You were halfway down the mountain. I thought you were dead."

"Did—did you see him?"

"Who?"

"The man with the cane."

"No. You weren't in the cabin, so I looked along the fire break. You were lying between the ridge and some trees. Lucky the ground was soft from the rain. What happened?"

"I don't know," I confessed, trying to sit up. "Someone came after me. With a cane. I thought—"

"You thought what?" Spensor demanded.

"That it was somebody I knew." I shook my head. It ached again. Bad. There was a cut on my shoulder oozing red through a layer of mud. The rest of me was pretty well caked with the brown slime.

Ray Spensor found some old rags in one of the cartons, and wiped my face and shoulders. "We ought to get you to a doctor," he said. "You're bleeding." He put a clean piece of cloth around the cut and under my arm, then slipped his sweater around my shoulders.

"Where's Toy?" I asked, trying not to squirm as he wiped more mud from my stomach and legs.

"Gone down the mountain. She threatened me with that Luger, but I knew she wasn't serious. I just couldn't leave you here."

"Thanks, Ray. What do we do now?"

"I'm going to carry you to the camp," he said, lifting me again. "They've got a doctor there."

Outside, the rain had faded into a fine mist in the late afternoon sky. He took a trail north of the cabin which zig-zagged down the face of the mountain. Mark Storm met us outside the temple. The big deputy took one look at me wrapped in Ray Spensor's letterman sweater, and he grimaced bitterly.

"Now what?" he boomed.

"I fell down the mountain," I said.

Mark glowered at the husky, pro football player who held me tight in his arms. "And I suppose he was waiting at the bottom to catch you."

"No, but I wish he had been." I decided to make the best of an awkward situation. "This is Rip's cousin, Lieutenant. All right, so I don't dig up suspects in a conventional manner. So put me in jail."

The deputy moaned. "Oh, how I wish I could. Come on, Spensor, I want to talk to you."

While I showered and had my shoulder wound bandaged, Mark questioned Ray Spensor in the hall outside the medical office. Apparently the Rams fullback told the deputy nothing about Toy Tunny's escapade because Mark asked about my missing clothes when he came inside.

"I gave everything else away," I said chidingly. "So

why not those, too. I'm a benevolent gal."

He leaned against a wall, shooting a side glance at the skinny, unclothed doctor who sat at his desk filling out a report of my accident. "If I thought you were serious," Mark said, "I'd give a donation to this dump just to keep you out of my county's hair for a while. What's the tab, Doc?"

"Flesh wound," the medical man said, not looking up. "Nothing serious."

"How about my injured vanity?" I asked, trying to hide myself in the letterman's sweater.

"It'll heal," the deputy countered. "Now what were you doing up on the mountain?"

The doctor left the room at Mark's nod.

"I was raising cane," I said, noticing a welt on the side of my right leg. I shoved myself off the examination table and stood up, smoothing the bulky sweater down over my hips. "Where's Fred Sims?"

"I dunno. Filing his story, I suppose." Mark tucked a cigarette in his mouth and lit it. "How many times must I repeat my question?"

"Oh, Mark," I snapped. "Stop trying to play big strong detective with me. What'd you dig out of Tunny?"

"A game of Scrabble."

"Don't pull the wool over my eyes, Lieutenant."

He glanced at my bare legs and grinned. "Right now you could use a little wool, but not over your eyes, sweetheart." He exhaled some smoke. "Your hypnotic theory was a flop. We questioned at least thirty different members. We even brought up a specialist from San Berdoo.

He says they may look like Barney Google, but they're happy as clams. Not one of them was in a trance or spell."

"You must have spent an illuminating afternoon."

Mark cocked his hat back and smiled. "I felt like a medical examiner in a French brothel."

"What'd they say about Angela Scali?"

"They all admitted she spent the last five or six months here. She was considered a holy princess. They didn't see much of her, except in the temple during worship. She was the symbol of peace and prosperity."

"I can believe that," I said. "She must have made a lot of money off her last picture. Tunny probably got a generous slice."

"We checked every available book, bank statement, even his safe. There's no indication of a theft or fraud perpetrated on Angela Scali. As far as we can tell she came here of her own free will."

"So where do you go from here?" I asked, thinking about Fred Sims and the incident on the mountain. I wanted to tell Mark about the man with the cane, but I couldn't. I wasn't sure about Fred. A hunch told me my assailant had been the crippled newsman. But I had to check it out myself.

"I'm going home," the deputy said, stubbing out his cigarette. "The San Berdoo men left hours ago. I hung around wondering what happened to you. I should have known you'd turn up in somebody's arms. Don't tell me there's a four-poster up in that cabin Spensor was talking about."

"Believe me, Lieutenant, there are four of everything. And I've got the welts to prove it. What are you going to do with Spensor?"

"Nothing—yet." Mark shoved his hat back on his head grimly. "I'll check out his story. I wish I could check yours out first. Want a ride back to town?" He turned toward the door.

"I have my own car," I said. "And speaking of firsts, I've got to dig up some clothes before leaving these hallowed grounds. Some county patrol officer might book me for speeding—without a license."

He shrugged dismally. "I fully expect a phone call before midnight."

After Mark had driven away in his Sheriff's car, I found Ray Spensor waiting for me in a room at the end of the medical building. His eyes lighted as I opened the door.

"Honey, you're positively magnificent," he said, moving toward me.

"I don't know how magnificent," I returned. "But I feel positively indecent wearing nothing but your sweater."

He snapped his fingers. "I've got an idea. Toy stole your clothes, so why not return the favor."

"What do you mean?"

"She has a separate apartment here on the grounds. And I have a key."

"Her things wouldn't fit me."

He nodded. "How about Angela Scali?"

"Sure," I said, studying the key ring he removed

from his pants pocket. "But where does she keep her clothes?"

There must have been fifty keys on his ring. He shot a knowing look at me and rattled them in his hand. "Leave that to me," he said. "Don't forget I brought her home this morning."

We walked outside. The rain had stopped and night was swiftly closing in over the mountains, dragging huge shadows along the ridges and valleys below Meadow Falls. Behind the medical building was a quadrangle with numerous individual apartments spaced intermittently about the grounds. Lights gleamed from most of the windows. Ray led me to one darkened apartment on the far edge. He inserted a key in the lock and opened the door.

"Here we are," he said. "Shrine of the Italian Angel."

Angela's small apartment was just that. A shrine. The walls were painted bright gold. A bronze, red-tongued dragon coiled from the ceiling. Candelabras gleamed. In one corner was a weird bust of Angela, head thrown back, mouth wide.

"Some layout," I said, entering slowly. "When's the floor show begin?"

"I thought you'd appreciate this," Ray said, following me inside. "When Angela was alive only directors were admitted."

"Did that include you?"

His square-jawed face reddened. "I worked at Meadow Falls this past summer with Rip. I was nothing more than an assistant. Rip made the grade though."

"With the Angel?"

"Sure." He closed the door and peeked through a window at the darkened quadrangle. "How long did you know Rip, Honey?"

"A few months, why?"

He turned, examining my legs that jutted beneath his letterman's sweater. "Did he ever mention Meadow Falls to you?"

"No."

"Did he ever talk about Angela Scali?"

"No, why do you ask?"

He slumped down on a bed in the corner, cocking one arm under his head. "There was something funny going on between Rip and Angela."

"What do you mean, *funny?*"

He had piercing brown eyes and they followed me as I moved toward a clothes closet.

"I don't know exactly," he said. "Something to do with this cult. I never got the details."

I opened the closet and picked through a row of dresses and sports clothes, finally settling on a black sweater and skirt. "What's going on between you and Toy Tunny?"

"Nothing." He said it rather flatly.

"She calls you baby."

"She calls everybody *baby*. She's a real mixed-up kid." As I crossed toward the bathroom, he reached up and pulled me down beside him on the bed.

"Hey!" I yelped.

"Honey," he said, leaning over me. "When I first saw you I nearly flipped."

"Careful or you're going to have me doing the same thing," I said uncomfortably.

His hands touched the sweater, fingers taut.

"You're beautiful, Honey."

"Ray." I pushed his hands away. "I'm a big girl and big girls have a lot more to get excited about than little girls. So please cut it out before I forget I'm a private detective."

He rolled over on the bed, forcing my arms up around his shoulders, his mouth lowering on mine.

"There's a button missing—here," he whispered.

"Ray—"

My lips felt his and they were restless and hard. There was a dimple in his chin and a small scar on his cheek.

"I'm going to give you ten minutes to stop that," I said.

"That's a tough sentence, Your Honor. I'm going to appeal."

"Twenty minutes," I breathed softly, then caught myself. "No, Ray, please—"

He opened another button. "Why is it a woman always says no when she means yes?"

"I'm serious, Ray, please."

He kissed me again, mouth brushing my cheek and ear and neck. Fire seared my legs. I jerked.

"Please, Ray!"

"I'm sorry about what happened in your apartment," he said "It was Toy's idea." His hands kept moving down my body. My arms stiffened around his shoulders.

"You don't have to explain," I said.

"I want to," he said. "She told me to kick in your kitchen door."

"Why?"

"She swore Rip's murderer was inside."

"Did you believe her?"

"I did until I found you lying on the floor." His huge shadow curved across the ceiling, blotting out the red-tongued dragon. I gritted my teeth, staring at the shadow, arms tight around his shoulders. Suddenly another shadow loomed into view.

Then a voice boomed, "Get up, Spensor!"

Ray's head snapped around. Thor Tunny stood next to the bed, red-rimmed eyes glowering down at us. Two other naked men stood behind the huge cult leader.

Tunny spat, "You're under arrest!"

Ray straightened. "What?"

"We just held a special election," the flame-haired leader said tautly. "Miss West has been chosen our new princess. You've just violated a serious code. Up!"

"You can't do this," Ray protested, fists doubling.

Before I could issue a warning, one of Tunny's musclemen knotted his fingers together and brought them down on the back of Ray Spensor's neck. The Rams player toppled to the floor soundlessly.

I leaped to my feet, gathering Ray's sweater around me, and headed for the door. But Tunny knocked me against the wall with his fist.

"You play rough, don't you," I stammered, holding my jaw. "Don't try to hold me here unless you want to wind up having your next meal in a county jail."

"You don't frighten me, Miss West," Tunny said, rubbing his knuckles against his hairy chest, eyes hot on the front of my sweater. "In these mountains I'm God. There is no law, but my own. Now, on your knees!"

"If you're rolling dice, okay. Otherwise you can take a flying leap at a Sputnik."

His biceps rippled. "Your humor fails to arouse me, Miss West. Fortunately you have a magnificent body which makes up for your lack of humility. This does arouse me. Greatly. Perhaps an hour in the Playground will change your tune."

"I quit playgrounds when I was in short skirts," I said. "Now get out of my way!"

Tunny didn't move. Neither did his two ape men who guarded the door.

"You are a princess now," Tunny said. "You must be indoctrinated into the cult. Come, my dear."

He extended his hand toward me. I grasped it firmly, twisted the arm around my back, and lunged forward. The huge cult leader flew up into the air, screaming angrily. Then suddenly his head crashed into the wall and he dropped, unconscious, onto the bed. Tunny's two apes moved toward him instinctively, mouths open. That gave me just enough room to make the door.

The quadrangle was pitch black now and a cool wind blew down from the mountaintop. I raced as fast as I could toward the temple, legs pounding. I hated to leave Ray Spensor behind, but I knew it was either him or me.

They'd chosen Angela Scali as their princess and she'd wound up with a seven-month blackout. Mine might last a year. Or longer. There was no doubt in my mind that the Playground was some sort of female torture chamber, designed to titillate some, and, as in the case of my former young client, terrorize others.

Chances of escaping the camp seemed slim. Even if my car was still parked by the temple, there seemed little chance the keys would be in the ignition. Then there was the thick-chested gatekeeper. He'd remember me and my bottle of suntan lotion.

All the way to the temple I kept wondering why Tunny wanted to keep me around. This afternoon I'd been ordered off the grounds. Now he wanted to erect a shrine in my honor. That's partially what he had in mind. The remainder came under the heading of intramural sports. I turned the corner of the temple at a dead run, the clatter of footsteps behind me in the quadrangle. An angry voice shouted. My car glistened in the darkness, parked near the temple's front steps. I flipped open the door and fumbled frantically at the dashboard. The keys were not in the ignition!

Another voice sounded in the night. I dropped to the ground and crawled under my convertible. From my vantage point, I saw a pair of shoes and naked legs bound into view. Then another. A door swung open and slammed closed.

"She's not here," a voice cried. It sounded like Adam Jason. "Spread out. Two of you take the road. Alert Drummond at the gate."

They began to scatter, moving away from the temple. A flashlight gleamed distantly, then faded. I waited for fully five minutes, until the sounds were all gone. The ground was icy cold on my bare legs as I crawled out and stood up. I listened. The falls crashed faintly up the valley, reminding me of Angela Scali and of the tree and the bloody bank.

I circled the car slowly, clutching Ray's sweater, listening intently for footsteps. At the corner of the temple a man moved out of the shadows passing only a few yards away from me. Apparently blinded by the darkness, he continued around the quadrangle without sounding an alarm.

Stealthily I crept around the individual apartments, keeping out of the quadrangle as much as possible. Finally I reached Angela Scali's place again. The door stood open. I peeked inside. Ray Spensor still lay sprawled face down on the floor. Tunny and his henchmen were gone.

I went inside and leaned over Spensor. Blood oozed from a cut on the back of his neck. In the bathroom I found a cloth and ran cold water over it. The pressure was low, so I peeled open the shower curtain and reached in to turn the handles.

That's when I noticed spots of red on the tile floor. But that wasn't all I noticed. A tiny piece of metal with five white stars on a bright blue field caught my eye.

I picked it up. There was a safety clasp on the back. It was a soldier's ribbon. And it was spattered with blood. I blinked. The ribbon represented the highest honor ever awarded an American military man. The Congressional Medal of Honor. I'd only seen one of these before in my life.

Newsman Fred Sims carried his as a good luck charm in the breast pocket of his coat.

EIGHT

The wet cloth brought Ray Spensor to his knees slowly, clutching the back of his neck, groaning.

"I'll take the penalty," he mumbled.

"What?"

"Fifteen yards. I was clipped."

I brushed hair from his eyes and helped him to his feet.

"You'll need more yardage than that," I said, glancing through the window. "We're surrounded."

He staggered to the door and snapped out the lights. "Where's Tunny?"

"I don't know. The last time I saw him he was breaking his head on the wall. They must have taken him to the dispensary."

Footsteps rattled outside in the quadrangle and we flattened against the wall.

"Did they hurt you, Honey?" he whispered.

"They had ideas. One was the Playground."

Ray exhaled audibly. "Dirty bastards."

"I got away, but they'd taken the keys to my car, so I circled back here to get you."

"Good girl. I know a way out."

"How, Ray?"

"Underground. There's a tunnel that leads beyond the main gate. Tunny had it built in case of an emergency. Come on!"

He took my hand. We dodged shadows in the quad, finally reaching the temple. The front doors were open. Ray guided me inside, staying close to an inside wall.

"I've got a telephone in my car," I whispered. "Maybe I could reach the San Berdoo Sheriff's office."

"Too risky."

We moved down a narrow staircase into a pitch-black space that smelled of orange blossoms and sweat.

"I don't like this," I confessed, holding his arm.

Ray snapped on a light. In front of us was a room built underground. There were metal slides and miniature merry-go-rounds and teeter-totters and swings.

"The Playground," I said. "But I don't understand—"

Ray gestured. "At first glance they look like they were made for kids, don't they? Take another look, Honey."

I did. And winced. Those machines weren't made for kids. . . . For adults, and *real* sick ones, at that.

"I—I don't believe it," I said.

"If they got you on one of those contraptions you would," Ray countered.

I shook my head dismally. "Are these Tunny's inventions?"

"No. Toy thought them up."

"What?"

"I told you she was a peculiar girl. She's completely warped."

"But she doesn't look—"

"I know," Ray said, shrugging his huge shoulders. "You can't explain something like this. It's just too crazy."

I studied his face carefully. "Toy said you spent some time down here, Ray. Can you explain that?"

"I had to, Honey. It was all part of my job. A great number of Tunny's disciples are maladjusted women with money. They come here seeking a new thrill. And they get it. From every which way. Including the pocket book."

"You mean they actually—"

"Of course," he said. "You know the type. In big cities they hire gigolos, male companions, male prostitutes. Here they get room service, access to the Playground, a chance to flaunt their bodies, and a religion to salve their twisted consciences. The nudist camp with a gimmick, that's Tunny's operation."

I glanced around at the weird machines. "I've heard of bizarre organizations, but this tops them all."

"Yeah," Ray answered, flicking off the light. "Don't think this murder of Angela Scali hasn't scared the daylights out of Tunny. He knows a thorough investigation could close him up. I'm surprised those deputies didn't run onto this room today."

"Maybe they did," I said, feeling his hand in the darkness again. "But they would have noticed—"

"They wouldn't necessarily. Those things are all detachable anyway. No doubt Tunny had them removed as soon as the Sheriff's men arrived."

Suddenly Ray bumped into something. He fumbled around for a moment, then swore. "Tunny's thought of everything. He's locked the tunnel door."

"What are we going to do, Ray?"

"I suppose we could try and climb the mountain."

"In the dark?"

He groaned. "No, that would be too dangerous. How about crossing the ignition wires on your car?"

"I'm game."

"Okay, let's go."

He led us back up the narrow staircase and into the temple. Candles flickered on the altar. My left hand still held the blood-spattered ribbon I'd found inside Angela Scali's shower. I kept wondering about Fred Sims. Had he been the man with the cane? Was this his war ribbon?

"It's raining again," Ray said, staring out the temple doors. "That's a break."

Drops sprayed down on us as we moved onto the stone steps. Lightning crackled in the distance. We reached my car safely. I began to feel uneasy. It didn't make sense that they wouldn't leave someone to watch my car or the temple.

Ray crawled under the dashboard and tore some wires loose.

"I've got a flashlight in the glove compartment," I whispered.

"No," he said. "They'd see us from a mile away."

I climbed in beside him and removed my auto phone.

I had difficulty reaching the mobile operator because of the mountains, but finally she came on the line. Before I could request the San Bernardino Sheriff's office something cracked under the dashboard. My phone went dead.

"Dammit," Ray said softly. "I pulled the wrong wire. Sorry, Honey."

"You cut my connection."

"I thought that was the hot wire from the battery. Got mixed up it's so dark."

I lowered the phone into the cradle and surveyed the darkness. "Fine time to pull the wrong wire. We might have had some help inside an hour."

"Don't worry. We'll get out of here."

"Hope so."

Thunder broke in the mountain sky, rattling across the valley angrily.

"The starter, Honey!" Ray yelled. "Try it now!"

I clamped it down to the floorboard, making the engine roar up into the night. Ray crawled out from under the dash and grasped the steering wheel.

"Let's get out of here!"

The convertible jerked forward, whirled around in front of the temple and headed toward the camp road.

"Turn on the lights," I said. "You're liable to hit somebody."

"I shouldn't," he returned, snapping them on, "but—"

Rain slashed at the windshield as we zoomed up the road, the wipers wedging two slim holes in the storm.

"Looks as if they might have given up the search," Ray said, squinting out of the side window.

"I hope so."

"There's still the gatekeeper."

I nodded.

When we reached the gate, our headlights illuminated the huge hairy-chested man standing before the barrier, waving his arms. Ray didn't slow up.

"Hey, what are you doing?" I shouted.

"We'll scare him out of the way."

"You'll hit the fence," I broke. "Those timber'll bend us into putty!"

At the last instant, Ray slammed on the brakes skidding to a stop a few feet from the camp's exit. The bald gatekeeper didn't waste any time yanking open my door. He reached in after me, but I kicked him in the throat and he fell back into some brush, cursing.

Ray Spensor leaped from the car and lifted the gate's heavy cross-beam out of its niche, then tossed it on the side of the road. But the gatekeeper caught Ray before he could swing open the gate. Bellowing like a wounded bull, Drummond swung Ray around as lightning zig-zagged down into the valley and exploded fiercely in a grove of trees beyond the fence.

Both men stiffened in their tracks as the fireball burst, outlining them hugely in the rain. Then Ray Spensor jabbed his right hand into the other man's face. The stocky gatekeeper didn't even flinch, but brought his own fist hard across Spensor's jaw. The football player dropped in the muddy road.

I climbed from the car. The gatekeeper leaped on the fallen man, gouging at his face with his fingernails. Ray kicked, rolled, grasped a small piece of a broken tree branch and swung savagely. The wood caught Drummond, splintering on his bald skull. The ponderous gatekeeper straightened, then fell hard in the middle of the road. Ray scrambled to his feet, stumbled forward and swung again. Blood spurted from the gatekeeper's head. He swung again wildly and missed. I caught his arm.

"You're going to kill him!" I shouted.

Ray Spensor stared at me, into the headlights, and shook his head. Rain streamed down over his face and shoulders. His mouth was bloody. He wiped his hand across his jaw dazedly, then tossed down the splintered branch, nodding.

We dragged Drummond into a shack beside the gate.

"He's hurt," I said. "We can't leave him like this."

"It was either him or us," Ray said grimly. "What do you think he would have done to you if he'd yanked you out of the car?"

"I don't think he would have split my skull. One crack on his noggin was enough, Ray."

"I—I'm sorry." He wiped at his bloody face. "I guess I lost my head for a second. He was trying to dig my eyes out."

I noticed a phone on the wall of the shack. It was a special extension without a dial, which obviously buzzed another phone somewhere in the camp when the receiver was lifted.

"Is the gate open wide enough for us to get through?" I asked.

Ray crossed to a window and looked out into the downpour. "Almost."

"Okay," I said. "Drive on through to the other side and wait for me."

"What are you going to do, Honey?"

"Notify somebody at the camp." I started for the phone.

He grasped my arm. "Don't! They'll be on our necks in two minutes!"

"We'll have to take that chance."

His eyes narrowed harshly. "Do you want to wind up in the Playground?"

"No," I said, "but I don't want to wind up as an accessory to a manslaughter either."

"That was an accident," Ray said, staring down at the unconscious gatekeeper.

"Sure it was an accident. An accident that you didn't kill him. Now drive that car through to the other side and re-lock the gate."

He hesitated, released his hand from my arm and swore. "All right, only it's your funeral."

Lightning stroked the dark sky again as Ray jogged back to the car, his head bent against the rain. He pushed the gate open wide enough, climbed behind the wheel and then shot an angry glance at where I stood in the shack's doorway. Finally he drove on through the opening.

I crossed to the telephone and lifted the receiver. After a moment, the connection snapped and a voice spoke curtly, "Yes, Drummond."

"Who's this?" I demanded.

"Adam Jason. Who—who's this?"

"Your blessing in disguise."

"Honey! Are you at the gate?"

"No thanks to you," I said.

"Where's Drummond?"

"He met with a little accident. You'd better send out your head fixer right away."

"Tunny's in a rage," Adam blurted. "He's frothing at the mouth."

"Give him a shot of anti-rabies serum and put him in a cage where he belongs."

"You nearly fractured his skull."

"He tried mine for size first. Listen, Adam, I really wanted to help you, but you're working for the wrong side. Take my advice and get out while the getting's good."

"What do you mean, Honey?"

"I just got a peek at your sports arena. Tunny had me scheduled for the main event. Believe me, your athletic program is about to blow up in your face."

"You're not sitting so pretty yourself. Your friend Fred Sims was here a few minutes ago. He says a warrant for your arrest has been issued through the Sheriff's office."

"You're lying, Adam."

"That's what you think. Sims was down in San Berdoo

early this afternoon. He came back in a rented car. The word is that some new evidence has cropped up in the Spensor murder that links you."

"I don't believe it."

A horn honked loudly. Ray was becoming impatient.

"Are you trying to detain me, Adam?"

"No, Honey. Listen, I'm fed up with Tunny and his tin god religion. I want out, but I'm afraid to make the break. I need your help."

I laughed grimly. "I've heard that song before, Adam. If you really want my assistance come to my office—fully clothed."

His voice lowered. "Please, Honey, don't leave me behind. I've got a feeling Tunny is going to—" The phone clicked on the other end.

"Hello, hello." I jiggled the hook. "Hello, Adam?" There was no response. I dropped the receiver in its cradle slowly, glancing around the small room. A shiver ran up my spine. I had a feeling Adam was in trouble, but I couldn't go back now. The risk was too great.

Ray Spensor came into the doorway, hair matted on his forehead from the rain, an angry scowl on his mouth.

"You going to stay here all night?" he demanded.

"Maybe," I said, studying the injured gatekeeper. "I'm worried about him, Ray."

"He's breathing, isn't he?"

I knelt down and felt Drummond's pulse. "Yes, but—"

He grasped my arm. "Come on!"

I jerked loose. "I've had enough strong arm, thank you. Now lay off!"

He shrugged, grimly wiping water from his eyes, and moved toward the door. "Okay, I'll go alone. I told you how Tunny feels about me. I'm not taking any chances."

"That's my car, buster!"

"I don't care whose car it is. I'm getting out."

He vanished in the darkness and downpour. I straightened, my gaze shifting to the unconscious man and then I looked around for a blanket to put over him. I found one in a corner closet. By the time I reached the door, the tail lights of my convertible were disappearing in the stormy night.

I bit my lips. I knew that was the last train. Rain spilled off the eaves, splattering on the shack porch. I turned and examined the gatekeeper again. He was bleeding badly from the gash in his skull. I was glad I hadn't left him.

After a few minutes another car drove up the road from the camp and parked outside the shack. I found a small hatchet in a drawer and raised it over my shoulder threateningly.

Footsteps dragged slowly outside. Then Fred Sims appeared, his cane bent under him, hat pulled low against the downpour. He stood in the doorway for a long instant surveying me, then his mouth slid into a wry smile.

"Who's carving?" he said.

I winced, realizing what he meant. I was half-crouched over an unconscious, bleeding man, a hatchet poised in my hand.

"Don't move, Fred. This instrument wasn't designed for turkeys—or a close shave."

"I can see that," he said lowly, frozen in the door. "You did a pretty bum job on him."

"He's not one of my most recent customers," I answered. "You want to try your luck?"

The newspaperman's head jerked awkwardly. "No, thanks. I use a Gillette myself. How are you fixed for blades?"

"Don't con me, Fred. What do you want?"

"You," he said quickly. "The Sheriff of Los Angeles County requests your presence for Thanksgiving dinner. He wants to roast you."

"He'll have to wait in line," I said, not moving an inch. "This is my busy season. I'm on everyone's holiday menu."

"Honey," he said," studying me in my hunched-over, half-naked position, "aren't you going about this case in a rather unorthodox manner?"

"For what I've got to work with I'm doing all right. Where do you stand, Fred?"

He squinted narrowly. "I scooped all the major papers. Now it appears I've got another first."

"It all depends upon your viewpoint," I said. "When you make the news you're always first."

He rapped his cane on the wood floor briskly. "Then you should have been a news reporter, Honey. You're generally always there, aren't you?"

"Depends," I said. "If I take a shower I usually pick my own stall. How about you?"

His face tightened perceptively. "I prefer baths myself. What's next on the agenda?"

"Mountain cabins," I said testily. "Ones with creaking doors and naked dames tied to the floor. How are you fixed for those?"

"They're running out of my ears," he answered, shifting slightly in the doorway, "since you're the one who's talking. Come on, Honey, relax."

I didn't move. "Is that what the president said to you when he pinned on the medal."

"What medal?"

"The one that has five stars and a blue field. Funny isn't it, Fred? Most guys receive that tribute posthumously, when they're already lying in a field."

Rain continued to slash behind him, filling the night with its noise and confusion.

His eyebrows lifted. "Now you're conning me, Honey. I didn't ask for the Congressional."

"Did Angela Scali?"

"Keep her out of this!"

I straightened slowly, still holding the hatchet. "You knew her, didn't you, Fred?"

"No!"

"You're lying, newsboy. You know you're lying."

His eyelids pinched so tightly they almost closed. "You're out of bounds, Honey!"

"Not in the football game I'm playing, I'm not. Where's your ribbon, Fred?"

His hand reached instinctively to his breast pocket, then lowered. "You're crazy, Honey. I come in here and you're bent over a bleeding man. What am I supposed to think?"

"What'd you think in that cabin when you—"

"What cabin?" he demanded angrily. "You having hallucinations?"

"Maybe."

"Then let's bury the hatchet!"

"Where, Fred?"

"I don't care where, just so long as it isn't in my back."

He made a quick move in my direction, snapping his cane down on the light switch. The room was plunged into black. I took one step, stumbled over the unconscious gatekeeper and sprawled on the floor. In the glare of a bolt of lightning, I saw Fred come toward me. I rolled, hooked my foot under his cane and flipped him over on his side. The newsman hit the floor with a vicious thud.

"You shouldn't have done what you did, Honey!" Fred shouted, above the storm's roar.

"Fred, so help me I'll use this hatchet if I have to. Don't move!"

He lifted himself on his left elbow, grunting from the effort, and swung at me with his cane. The tip grazed my sleeve.

"Fred, I'm warning you!"

He swung again. This time I caught the piece of hickory in mid-air and ripped it from his hands.

"You'd like to kill me, wouldn't you?" he shouted.

"Fred, you're out of your mind!"

I threw his cane against the wall, then dashed out the door. Two sets of headlights were moving up the road from the camp. I slipped behind the wheel of Fred's car and started the engine. It was a sleek, new sedan and still smelled fresh from the factory.

I pulled through the gate quickly, skidding on the muddy road, and turned toward the Mountain Highway. Rain teemed down, blinding me, slashing over the windshield in never-ending sheets. Thunder exploded violently in the night.

I was almost too stunned to cope with the storm. The gate shack incident with Fred Sims had been too much. Again he'd come at me with his cane. Again he'd tried to beat my brains out. Fred Sims. It seemed utterly impossible after all we'd been through together.

The headlights dwindled behind me and disappeared. I reached the Mountain Highway and turned into the downhill lane. At the first big curve I clamped down on the brakes. My foot sank to the floorboard. The sedan careened around the curve, skidding over the white line. My heart leaped into my throat. The brakes were gone.

NINE

There was a ripping crash as the sedan struck a guardrail on the downhill side of the highway, twisting back across the slick pavement, skidding out of control.

I tried the hand brake, but the metal handle came loose in my fingers. The cable was severed!

The grade at this point was perilously steep and narrow, carved sharply from the mountains. A cliff swung into my headlight's glare, rising straight and rocky in the rain. The wheel twisted in my hands.

Crash! The right front fender grazed the bluff, shooting up a shower of stones and pebbles that ricocheted off the windshield.

Another set of headlights loomed in front of me as the highway straightened for a few yards before another curve. They sliced ominously through the furious downpour, moving up the mountain slowly on the downhill side of the white line.

I was in the wrong lane! The wheel wouldn't

respond as the sedan skidded again on the wet pavement, veering out toward the guardrail. I snapped it viciously and the car spun sideways directly into the oncoming lights, grazing the rail, metal rending and tearing against the steel guard.

My hands flew instinctively to my face as the other vehicle's horn blared wildly, lights looming like two angry eyes. Suddenly the windshield seemed to explode and something ripped past my head with an ear-splitting frenzy. The seat jerked, tore loose from its mountings, throwing me hard toward the dashboard. My cheek brushed against the steering wheel as it twisted sideways mashing me down on the floor. The car spun violently, tipped, rolled, the sound of its death splintering around me in a hideous roar of steel and glass.

Then it was over, and there was nothing to hear except the rain and a slowly turning wheel that grated somewhere on a broken axle.

I felt around slowly, hardly able to believe I was still alive, not convinced in the futile darkness that life did exist in my bruised body. The broken steering column was bent around me like a pretzel. That much I could feel in the dark. I could feel, too, that the car was tilted forward on its frame as if the front end had dug a gaping hole in the ground, or was hanging downward into some awesome void.

By the time I'd unscrambled myself, I heard the distinct clatter of footsteps running hard on wet asphalt.

Then a voice cried out anxiously in the night, "Hey! Hey! Hey, down there, are you all right, for God's sake?"

I knew then why the car was tipped so severely. I crawled from under the battered dashboard and felt rain slamming down on my face. The door on the driver's side was gone and beneath its opening was a wide, seemingly unending space. I was over the side of the mountain.

"Is anybody alive down there?" the voice rose again.

"Yes!" It surged from my throat.

A flashlight cone erupted in the dark, spilling over the sedan, lighting my face through the persistent rain. More footsteps rang on the highway.

"What's happened?" another voice demanded.

"A car went out of control. Nearly hit me. Somebody's alive. Look at that, will you!"

A man swore. "The guardrail went clean through the front and rear windows. We'd better get some help fast before that damned thing breaks!"

I was beginning to get the picture. I'd missed the other vehicle, but the guardrail had apparently snapped and punctured my car like a sausage on a skewer. That was all that was holding me from a horrifying plunge down the mountain.

"Hey, down there!" the voice lifted again. "Are you hurt?

I felt around. Everything seemed to be in the right place. There was no hot rush of blood. No twisted arms or legs.

"I think I'm all right," I returned.

"How many are you?"

"Just one!" I answered, staring up into the light and rain. "Can you get me out of here?"

"It's a woman!" the other man yelled. "Good God!"

They seemed to be standing on the edge of the road about twenty feet above me. The broken guardrail slanted down in the light's arc, stabbing through the rear window and snaking around the sedan's frame.

"Can you get me out?" I repeated, wiping drops from my eyes and feeling for the first time an ache in my right arm.

"What are we going to do?" one man questioned dazedly. "She's hanging by a thread. Any more weight'll send her crashing."

The light shifted, spraying on the twisted guardrail.

"There's a rope in the back of my truck. Maybe we could drop it down to the one side where the door's gone."

The other man swore. "Hurry!"

Footsteps clattered again, melting in the downpour. I had a fairly good idea what they had in mind. Drop a rope, hoping that I could reach it and make a tie around my waist, then they'd pull me to safety. There was only one drawback to that solution. The opening was on the downside of the sedan. I'd have to risk leaning out into that hideous dark void to reach the rope. I inched my way toward the opening.

Suddenly the car lurched and I froze. It swayed back and forth for an instant, then stopped.

"Hurry up!" the man with the flashlight shouted. "The rail's beginning to go!"

I held my breath and tried to think of anything but the mountain and the two men and the black void below. My mind centered on Meadow Falls. Who could have tampered with the brakes? Somebody must have drained most of the fluid from the master cylinder, leaving just enough pressure to last until the highway. But that didn't make sense. No one knew I was going to steal Fred's car. Not even Fred himself. Unless—

"Here!" The other man appeared in the glare of the flashlight and bent over, gripping a rope in his hands. "Hey, down there! I'm going to drop this thing as near as I can to you. Try and twist it around your wrists or something. We'll pull you clear."

"How much do you weigh?" the man with the flashlight demanded.

"A hundred and twenty pounds."

The rope tumbled down in the cone of light, landing first on the rear of the car, then sliding near the opening.

"Lower!" I cried.

They let out more slack. The rope twisted awkwardly in the driving rain, swinging out and beyond me like a pendulum on a grandfather clock. Then a gust of wind blew it toward me. I caught my breath, reached as far as I possibly could, felt the car lurch again, felt rain beading on my outstretched hands, and caught the dangling rope.

In the next instant as metal began to rend, as the car began to slide out from under me in the driving downpour, I could feel my head bursting, pulse pounding, rope slipping through my fingers. The light vanished and I felt myself crashing against rock, scraping against it, hearing the sound of the sedan falling down the mountain, seeing the blur of its gas tank exploding in the night.

A hand caught me viciously, tearing at my hair, digging into my scalp. Another slipped around my shoulders. They dragged me up onto the edge of the mountain, both men panting heavily, arms linked around my aching body. We fell in a heap on the road.

Headlights loomed in the dark, casting wet shadows over us. One man scrambled to his feet, helping me up. He was tall and thick-shouldered and a cap was perched on his head. His eyes widened as he stared at me in the glow of the oncoming headlights.

Ray Spensor's letterman's sweater was torn wide open down one side.

"Hey," he said awkwardly. "You—you ain't dressed."

"That," I said, "is the understatement of the year."

A Sheriff's car from San Bernardino arrived twenty minutes later. Aside from a number of other statements made by my two rescuers and a few cocky, grinning-faced deputies, I wound up in the Sheriff's station with a robe, a cup of coffee and a sour-faced Mark Storm. He didn't even bother with my lack of wearing apparel. He started right in on my lack of horse sense.

"Honey," he blared, "you use your head like it was stuck through a piece of canvas in a baseball throwing booth at a carnival side show."

"That's my occupation, Lieutenant," I said, sipping at my coffee. "When somebody winds up, I dodge."

"Yeah, well dodge this. Some deputies broke into

your office late this afternoon. They found the missing keys to the steam roller that crushed Rip Spensor."

"What?"

"We got another anonymous tip. Apparently from a man. They found your office securely locked, including the windows. So, start dodging."

I shook some water out of my hair. "But, Mark, you know that I didn't—"

"I don't know anything. Fred Sims called me from Meadow Falls after you stole his car. He said the man you left lying inside the gate shack will live, but he's got a nasty gash on his skull. What was the matter, the hatchet too blunt to finish the job?"

I stiffened, gripping the robe. "Now wait a minute, Lieutenant, I don't—"

"You don't what? Thor Tunny's nursing a head as big as a Chinese gong. You went on quite a spree after I left, didn't you?"

"Spree?" I hurled. "I was lucky to get out of that sex trap alive. What were you doing while you were there? Playing tiddly-winks? Did you bother to examine the fancy machines beneath the temple? Did you look inside Angela Scali's shower stall?"

"What machines? What stall?"

I groaned. "And I suppose Fred's sterling telephone call included how I tried to crease his noggin, too?"

"Of course."

"Did he bother to tell you how he cracked me half a dozen times with his cane?"

Mark pushed his hat back angrily. "What was he supposed to do? Stand by while you carved him up like a Christmas goose?"

"I'm talking about earlier this afternoon," I said. "Up in that cabin on the mountain. I didn't take that high dive for nothing. Mr. Fourth Estate worked me over, but good."

"Hold it, Honey. You know Fred wouldn't do anything like that."

"Thanks, Lieutenant," I said harshly. "Fred wouldn't, but I would. Is that it?"

"I didn't mean—"

"You don't know what you mean, Lieutenant. That's the trouble. You get in the middle of a case and you start taking pot shots at every stray suspect who comes along, except the right one." I tossed him Ray Spensor's torn letterman's sweater. "Take a look in the left hand pocket."

He studied me for an instant, then shoved his hand into the opening."

"What's this?" he demanded, removing the blood-spattered ribbon.

"Don't tell me you've never seen one before?"

"It—it's a Congressional." He indicated the dark spots. "What happened here?"

"Fortunately, I didn't wind up in a crimson-colored basket or you would have blamed me. I found it in Angela Scali's shower stall at the camp."

Mark twisted the ribbon around in his fingers. "These are blood stains, all right."

"Thank you, Lieutenant. I was afraid you were going

to say they were the remains of a sand painting made by an early American Indian."

The deputy brushed at his face thoughtfully. "You—you're not kidding about this?"

"Wise up, Mark. Somebody obviously murdered Angela Scali, then returned to her apartment and washed off his bloody clothing. The ribbon must have dropped from the killer's pocket when he wasn't looking."

"But—but that doesn't make sense," Mark stammered. "Who'd carry one of these in his pocket?"

"Fred Sims," I said.

"Honey, are you out of your mind?"

"Maybe. It's worth investigating, isn't it?"

Mark tossed the ribbon in the air and caught it savagely. "But Fred was with us this morning!"

"How long was I unconscious? Three, four hours? When'd Fred show up at my apartment?"

"A few minutes before you woke up," the deputy said tightly. "But that still doesn't prove—Fred has no motive!"

"Do I?"

"Well, no, but—"

"Lieutenant, the man who came up to that mountain cabin limped. He walked with a cane. He sounded like Fred. He acted like Fred."

"Why didn't you tell me this before?" Mark's face was crumpled as if it had been beaten.

"Because I couldn't believe it, either. Not until after I found that ribbon. Not until after he attacked me again in the gate shack."

Mark grimaced. "These things can be purchased in service stores, you know."

"Sure," I said. "The same way missing steam roller keys can be purchased in a dime store. It's not that easy, Lieutenant. You've got to show proof you're a holder of the medal."

He tossed his hat on a desk and circled the room quietly, then said, "How could those keys have been planted in your office with the door and windows locked?"

"Some people do carry skeleton keys," I said wearily. "They seldom pack spare Congressional ribbons."

He stopped, wiping at his rain dampened face. "All right. I'll buy the plant in your office. I did anyway."

"Lieutenant, you amaze me," I said sarcastically. "I thought for sure you were going to produce a set of my fingerprints taken off the wheel of that steam roller."

"Don't stretch me, Honey."

"Mark, do you think I jumped with joy when I found that ribbon in Angela Scali's shower?"

"You sound happy enough."

I laughed grimly. "Take it for what it's worth. I still can't believe Fred murdered Angela Scali—or Rip Spensor. But, as I said, it's worth investigating."

Mark was sick inside. I could see that. As sick as any man could be without messing up the floor. He straightened, swallowing hard. "What about these machines you were talking about?"

I told Mark about the Playground. His face grayed. "If we can prove this," he said, "Tunny'll end up in another kind of camp. With numbers plastered on his chest instead of suntan lotion."

"The gimmicks are removable, Mark," I said. "You'll never get him unless you pull a surprise raid."

"We'll work it out through this office," he said, replacing his hat grimly. "Right now I've got a personal call to make."

"Fred Sims?" I asked.

"Maybe." He crossed to the door. "You say you think somebody drained the master cylinder on Fred's car, huh?"

"Either that or the nut was loosened enough to allow leakage every time the brakes were applied. No mistake about the hand brake. The cable was hacksawed."

He nodded grimly. "I'll let you know."

After Mark left, I borrowed a dress and a coat from a blonde telephone operator who worked in the Sheriff's building and walked outside into the chill, misty night. A clock on a bank at the corner chimed 10 o'clock as I crossed to a cab stand. Then a familiar convertible pulled up beside me, a handsome unshaven face peering through the window.

"Taxi, lady?" the man said, grinning warmly.

"Ray," I stammered. "Where—where the devil have you been?"

"Circling a mountain," he said, a chagrined look creeping around his mouth. "I understand you took a short cut."

"'Just about as short as they come," I answered,

climbing in beside him. "How'd you find out?"

He lifted my auto phone. "I got it working again. The Sheriff's office told me." He shook his head. "I'm sorry, Honey. If I hadn't left you—"

"That wasn't exactly heroic, Ray."

He bit his lips. "I know. I'd like to make it up to you if I could."

"Okay," I said. "This agent of Angela Scali's, the one Toy Tunny was talking about. Sol Wetzel. Do you know where he lives?"

"Sure."

"Will you take me there?"

He touched the tip of my nose and winked. "It's your car."

"Glad you finally remembered," I said, unable to stop the smile that came into my face. "First I'll need to make a stop at my apartment in Long Beach. I'm lost without your letterman's sweater."

"You're never lost, Honey," he said pulling out onto the highway and pointing my convertible toward Riverside. "Chart the course, commander!"

"Alamitos Bay. And don't spare the horses."

He grinned, turned south toward the freeway and drew me nearer. "It's a long ride," he said. "I might get cold."

I switched on the heater. "You'll do all right."

"Killjoy!"

When we reached my apartment, I showered hurriedly, climbed into a black sheath and suede pumps and wound some pearls around my throat. Then I outlined my mouth with pale pink lipstick, swept my hair back to one side and we continued on to Hollywood.

Angela's agent had a place in Box Canyon with a pool and a spectacular view of the surrounding hills. A number of cars were parked in the driveway and lights blazed inside the low-slung ranch-style house. The sound of bongo drums and castanets greeted us.

"Sounds like a party," Ray said stepping from the car. The open front door led us into a cloud of cigarette smoke and people who were clapping and stamping to a weird rhythm. Sweat streamed down one man's face as he stared across the room. Another licked at his mouth as he clapped. At the far end of the room the lights had been dimmed so I could only faintly distinguish the frantic outline of a woman dancing. She whirled, throwing up her arms, wriggling her hips.

Her dance couldn't have been more suggestive.

She was stark naked.

Dark arrows had been painted on her white body, swirling around her legs and breasts, all pointing in one direction.

"Holy smokes," Ray whispered. "Look at that!" I looked. So did the nude dancer. She stared down at her own body, hands flailing about her thighs, legs trembling.

Suddenly she fell to the floor, writhing, screaming, groaning.

The drums stopped.

The man who had been beating the bongos tore off his shirt and lifted the dancer into his arms.

'The pool!" he cried.

The room erupted in a frenzy of shouts and waving arms. They crowded toward French doors that lead out to the pool area, the nude dancer thrashing wildly in the bongo player's grasp.

I turned to say something to Ray Spensor, but he was gone. Somebody brushed against me. The sweaty-faced man grabbed me about the waist.

"Hey!" I yelled.

He started peeling me like I was a banana.

I planted a toe in his stomach and he fell back. Two others took his place, hoisting me in their thick hands. I kicked, squealed, bit and punched to no avail. They carried me out to the pool where the nude dancer was being mauled by a dozen different hands as they swung her out over the water.

That was when I saw her face for the first time.

It was Toy Tunny!

But I saw something else, too.

The gleaming blade of a switchknife rose over Toy's pudgy frame. And descended.

TEN

I screamed.

But the sound was lost in the wild orgy of hands and shouts by the pool.

The knife lowered to Toy's stomach, the tip nearly touching her skin as she swung loosely in the network of arms.

"Cut her!" somebody cried.

"Rip her to pieces!" shouted another.

I couldn't believe my eyes. Toy's teeth were bared in her round face, a smile etched in her red lips.

"Cut me!" she echoed.

The man with the knife lowered the gleaming tip a fraction and the blade sliced a faint line across Toy's stomach. The crowd thundered their approval. The arms lifted, hurling the chunky girl into the water.

"Who's next?" the bongo player shouted, staggering drunkenly on the edge of the pool. He held the knife in his right hand, waving it ceremoniously. They carried me to him.

"A blonde virgin!" the cry went up.

"Cut her!" came the echo.

Hands jerked down the zipper on the back of my dress. I'd had about enough. One of my heels flicked, catching a red-faced man in the neck. He toppled into the pool, choking horribly. Another caught a knee in his eye. I saved the best for last. The bongo player lunged for me. He had wavy black hair and a thin mustache. I poked my fist halfway between. His nose twisted from the impact, blood spurting from the nostrils. He dropped the knife, an anguished cry spurting from his lips. Hands slipped out from under me. I caught my balance, straightened and drove another fist into the bongo player's mid-section. He did a deep-knee bend, exhaling painfully and collapsed on the rim of the pool.

The crowd shrank back, eyes wide in their drunken, sweating heads, mouths open. The soundless moment that followed seemed reminiscent of a funeral after all the words have been said. I broke it harshly.

"You sadistic apes," I said, through my teeth. "You ought to be hung by your toes."

The man I'd pushed into the pool bobbed to the surface, spouting water like a baby whale. In the pool lights I could see Toy climbing up a metal ladder.

One man bent over the deflated bongo player, shooting angry eyes at me. "Are you mad?" he demanded.

"No," I said. "But I'm willing to take lessons. Is that what you people are giving around here?"

"This—this was all in fun," the bongo player stammered, clutching his ribs.

"If this is fun," I answered, casting hot eyes on the silent crowd, "then the morgue's full of it. Next time rent a cemetery."

Toy Tunny advanced on me, shaking water from her arrow-painted body, fists curled angrily. "How'd you get here?" she demanded.

"I followed one of your arrows," I said, staring at her knife-creased stomach. "You'd better put something on that."

"It's only a scratch, you idiot," she slammed harshly. "Why don't you keep your nose where it belongs?"

"I was," I said, "until two of your sweaty friends decided it needed powdering. Where's your Luger, Miss Tunny? You look positively naked without it."

She brushed at her rounded hips, shifting her gaze at the crumpled, bleeding bongo player. "Sol, this is the dame I was telling you about. The female shamus."

Sol groaned. "The—the party's over everybody. Go home," he stammered. "Go home."

They dispersed slowly, shaking their heads, growling under their breaths. I looked around for Ray Spensor, but still couldn't see him. Toy Tunny picked up a towel from a nearby lounge chair and wrapped it around her abundant doll-shaped frame. Then she bent over the still-gasping bongo player.

"You all right, baby?" she asked.

"Yes, yes," he groaned. "Just get her out of here."

"That won't be so easy, Sol," Toy said, helping him to his feet. "She's here about Angela. You'd better talk to her."

So this was Sol Wetzel, the Italian Angel's illustrious agent. I began to get a picture. One with a fancy frame around it, gold-leafed with a wide border. I yanked up my zipper and gestured toward the French doors.

"After you," I said.

Helping Sol Wetzel was no easy task for Toy Tunny. Sol was a tall man, sturdily built, and strong. He leaned on the chunky shoulders of the towel-covered woman as they staggered inside. They crossed to the bar.

"Okay, Miss West," Toy said, pouring Sol a drink. "Let's have it."

"Where are my clothes—and gun?"

She cocked her thumb toward a door. "In Sol's bedroom. You're welcome to them. They don't fit worth a darn. And that pink pearl-handled job is a little too fancy for me."

Wetzel moaned, mopping his nose with a handkerchief. "What else do you want?"

I surveyed the drink-and-ash-tray-littered living room. "Your version of Angela Scali's disappearance."

"The newspapers carried my story seven months ago. Don't you read?"

"I read what you said. Now I'd like the truth."

"That was the truth."

I noticed an Academy Award Oscar on the fireplace mantel. "Come on, Mr. Wetzel, you're not playing the bongo drums now. You're way off-key. You knew Angela Scali was at Meadow Falls."

"I did not!"

"You're a bald-faced liar."

"Prove it, Miss West. Do you think I'd let ten percent of a million dollars slip through my fingers just like that?"

"Maybe," I said.

"No maybes about it," he growled. "The Angel was my meal ticket. I had a six-picture deal cooking for her when she disappeared."

I crossed to the mantel and removed the statuette. "What happened to all the money she made from her last movie, Mr. Wetzel?"

"How the hell should I know?" He glanced at Toy nervously.

"Didn't I read somewhere that Angela Scali made close to a half million off *The Big Pebble?*"

"That—that's right."

"Didn't I also read where her money mysteriously vanished at the same time she did?"

He swallowed some of his drink and choked. "Yes. Yes, the police conjectured at the time that she took it with her."

"Did she?"

"How should I know?" he hurled, snatching the Oscar from my hands.

"What about that, Miss Tunny?" I asked. "Did the Angel show up at Meadow Falls carting a bag full of money in her lily-white hands?"

Toy laughed. "She had some money, sure. You're chasing a rainbow, Honey. The cult's a non-profit organization. You can check our books. We haven't received a donation over a thousand dollars since we opened."

"I'm sure you haven't," I said. "But what you've taken is a different story."

"I resent that," Toy cried, shoulders tensing.

"And I resent the hanky-panky you two are playing," I said. "This afternoon you waylayed me in a cabin above Meadow Falls, Miss Tunny. At the time you accused Mr. Wetzel here of murdering Rip Spensor—and Angela Scali."

Wetzel whirled toward the pudgy brunette. "What?"

"She's lying, Sol," Toy said, face reddening. "Why would I accuse you?"

His eyes narrowed. "Are you playing me for a sucker, Toy?"

"Shut up, Sol!"

"I always thought you were. You didn't come here to conjure any spirits. You purposely led her here, didn't you?"

"Don't be a sap, Sol!"

I jumped at the opportunity, moving between them. "No, don't be a sap, Sol. Toy said you were in love with Angela. That you hated any rivals. Especially Rip Spensor."

His mouth cinched tightly. "She knows I didn't love Angela. But she knows somebody who did."

"Who?" I demanded.

"Let me show you something, Miss West," Wetzel said, moving toward his bedroom door. "This'll probably surprise hell out of you."

He disappeared, leaving Toy alone with me in the living room. The towel-clad doll scowled, poured herself a drink and gulped it quickly.

"What's happened to your friend Ray Spensor?" I asked, watching her carefully.

"Drop dead!"

"He came up here with me, then pulled one of his vanishing acts. He seems famous for that."

"Ray is famous for a lot of things," she said tartly. "You'll learn that in time. Especially if you belong to the female sex."

"And what's that supposed to mean?"

"In a word, Miss Private Eye, Ray's a lover. He makes more yardage in a boudoir than he does on a gridiron, if you get what I mean."

"How did he do with Angela Scali?"

"Are you kidding?" she snickered. "The Angel wouldn't have anything to do with Ray Spensor. Nor with Fred Sims, either."

"What?"

"Fred Sims," she said flatly. "You know him, don't you? The crippled newspaperman."

I tried to keep from reacting at the mention of Fred's name, but I couldn't help the shock in my face and eyes.

"Yes, I know him," I said. "How did Fred fit with Angela Scali?"

She shrugged. "He met her once on an assignment from his paper. That's the story I got. I guess the poor guy fell pretty hard."

"How do you mean, *fell?*"

"Goggle-eyed, short-of-breath. You know the bit. He was panting on her heels for months."

"You mean while she was at the camp?"

"Before and after," Toy said. "He's a creep with that gimpy leg. I don't know how Angela stood him."

"But I don't understand," I said. "If Fred knew Angela Scali was at Meadow Falls why didn't he break the story?"

Her smile was edged with sarcasm. "Miss West, you really surprise me. You still have the mistaken idea the Angel was spirited to Meadow Falls, don't you? She wasn't. She came of her own accord. And for a very good reason."

"And what was that?"

"She was sick of the life she was leading," Toy said. "It was as phony as a nine-dollar bill and she knew it. She hated the people and the pace and the front she had to maintain. Can you blame her?"

"I can't if it's true," I answered. "But why didn't Fred Sims break the story?"

"Because she asked him not to. Fred would do anything Angela said. He was that far gone."

I nodded. The noose was tightening around Fred's scrawny neck. In a way I still couldn't believe it. The whole thing seemed too fantastic. I hoped that what Sol Wetzel had to show me would throw some light on the situation. I turned toward the closed door.

"What's keeping him?" I asked.

She shrugged. "I don't know. Sol's another one who needs a psychiatrist's couch. He's an abominable liar."

"You mean he was in love with Angela?"

"Like a puppy dog. Listen, what I told you this afternoon sticks. I still think Sol is guilty. Did you see him with that knife? He's ready for the nut house."

I thought of the weird machines back at Meadow Falls. If those were Toy's inventions she was calling the kettle black.

"You begged him to cut you," I said.

"Of course I did," she argued. "I saw you come in with Ray. I wanted to prove how crazy he was."

"If that's true you took quite a risk."

She snickered again. "He wouldn't have hurt me in front of that crowd."

"Toy?" Wetzel's voice floated up from behind his bedroom door. "Come here a minute."

She stiffened. "I'd better see what's the matter."

Toy Tunny gathered the towel around herself and crossed to the door, disappearing inside. After an instant, the lock clicked. I was tempted to eavesdrop, then discarded the idea. They were both too clever to say anything when the two of them were alone. I snapped on a portable radio near the bar and tried to pick up a midnight newscast. The speaker shuddered with rock and roll and the day's most popular ballad, "Mack, The Knife." I shook my head. A fiendish killer was No. 1 on the Hit Parade. Switchblade knives had taken the place of hearts and flowers. No longer were there songs about love and marriage. This season it was mayhem and masochism.

Toy came out of Wetzel's bedroom, finally, closing the door behind her. She switched off the radio, took a cigarette from a pack on the bar and lit it casually. Then,

"Sol can't find what he's looking for. He's mad as hell. Even talking to himself."

Suddenly Wetzel's voice lifted inside the room. "You fool!" he cried.

"What's that?" I asked.

"Like I said. He's talking to himself. He's as mad as a hatter."

Wetzel's voice continued, "You think you're smart, don't you? Well you're not. You're a fool!"

"He's speaking to somebody," I said.

"There's nobody in there," Toy countered, puffing at her cigarette. "He's had too much to drink."

"I'll kill you!" the agent's voice rose defiantly. "If you come closer, I'll kill you!"

I started toward the door, but Toy stopped me.

"He's just flipping his lid," she said. "I told you he was ready for the wraparound coat."

"No!" Wetzel cried. "No! No! No!"

I brushed Toy out of the way and bolted through the door. Sol Wetzel was lying across a bed in the corner, his legs twisted under him. A door to the rear of the room stood open, swinging in the wind. I bent over the agent. His eyes stared at me glassily. The switchblade knife protruded from his chest.

ELEVEN

Wind blew the outside door, banging it against the wall, blowing papers from a desk and scattering them over the dead man. I bent over him. There was no pulse and his eyes were wide, full of horror. Blood flowed from the wound, running down his chest, staining the bed.

Toy Tunny came into the room and screamed, hand crushing to her mouth. The wind blew again, toppling books from a shelf, crashing them down on a tape recording machine and knocking one of its reels spinning across the floor.

"Where's my gun?" I demanded.

She gestured at a chair in the corner. I crossed quickly, removing the revolver from under the sweater Toy had taken from me, and then stepped through the door into a narrow walkway behind the house. A half moon gleamed faintly through fleecy clouds, bathing an embankment above the walkway with a purplish smear of light. I glanced to my left. A cement-block wall about ten feet high circled a small patio that still held puddles from the day's downpour. A Chinese lantern swung idly in the wind, casting shadows across the wet squares.

To the right was a narrow passage swinging around toward the garage and driveway where my convertible stood, grimly silent in the windy night. I moved slowly down the walkway, hand gripping my revolver, legs taut. At the edge of the garage, I whirled at the sight of something along the bank above my head. A big brown object sprang down at me, spinning weirdly in the light, bouncing on the cement, caroming off a post directly into my path.

I kicked wildly, darting back into the garage, then caught my breath. It was a tumbleweed! The crazily-turning, gnarled growth blew against my convertible, bounding over the hood and across Sol Wetzel's garden, vanishing down the hillside.

I felt around for a light switch. Trees swayed across the driveway, their branches thrashing loudly. Far below the ridge, I could see the lights of other houses, fanning out in the canyon.

Sol Wetzel's killer couldn't be far, unless he'd had a car waiting. I had a hunch he was nearby. I could almost feel his presence in the pitch-black garage. My gun hand trembled as I moved out onto the driveway, heels clicking on the asphalt. Wind whipped at my hair, blowing it across my face and eyes. I started toward my convertible. The door was open on the driver's side. I moved around the car cautiously, gaze shifting from the house to the road behind me. A dog howled across the canyon, a lonely cry in the night. I stopped, listening intently. A tree branch snapped, shuddered, spraying leaves across the driveway.

I froze, staring up toward the embankment again. Nothing moved, except weeds high on the cliff above the house. Then something rattled on the asphalt behind me. I whirled. A piece of paper blew up in my face, darting skyward, turning eerily in the cloud-etched sky above my head.

I thought about fairy tales I'd read when I was a child. About monsters and dragons lurking in the grassy hills when night descended over the land. Somewhere a murderer lurked, woven into the darkness like an evil creature from Grimm's. I knew I had to find him before he found me. But where? My legs turned me in a full circle, then back again. A tree branch grazed against my face, its chill wet fingers brushing ominously. I darted around the car, stopping by the open door, and inhaled deeply.

This was one person I didn't want to meet in a dark alley, or a night-pitched driveway. He'd already killed as violently as anyone could. A metal machine weighing three tons had crushed the life out of Rip Spensor. A knife and a rope were the tools of violence exercised on Angela Scali. Now Sol Wetzel. Stabbed in the heart.

I reached inside and lifted my auto phone, mechanically placing a call to my office. Wind blew new rain on my forehead and my eyes searched the driveway again as the number rang.

Charley April intercepted quickly, "Honey West, private—"

"Charley," I interrupted, "have you ever been alone and felt like the last person alive in the whole wide world?"

"Constantly, Springtime. Where are you?"

"On the side of a mountain. It's raining and I'm scared, Charley."

"You need help?"

"In the worst way," I said. "Charley, I like you when you smile."

"Honey, for God's sake, I'm not smiling. Where are you?"

"Box Canyon," I said, brushing drops from my nose. "High up on the Hollywood side. A man's just been murdered."

"Who?"

"Nobody you know, Charley."

"I know a lot of people, Springtime. Don't be elusive."

"A guy named Sol Wetzel. Hollywood agent up until five minutes ago."

Charley grunted. "Sure, I know him. Wetzel was one of my best clients. He blew more than twenty grand on the ponies at Hollywood Park this past summer."

"You serious?"

"You know I am with you, Springtime. He was a light spender season before last. A grand at the most. This year he busted wide open. At horse-playing, he was a dud. I told him so, but he wouldn't quit."

"Charley, you're an angel," I said, my gaze shifting toward the garage. "What would I do without you?"

"Maybe you'd talk sense," he blared. "Gimme the address and I'll phone the Sheriff's office."

A figure suddenly moved out of the shadows near the garage.

"Too late," I said numbly and hung up.

Ray Spensor walked toward the car, hand shielding his eyes against the new drizzle.

"Honey?"

"Hold it where you are, Ray!"

He stopped. "What's the matter?"

"Where'd you go?"

"For a walk," he said. "That smoke in there was too much for me."

"Have you seen anyone?"

"Sure, I saw a whole bunch of people come out of the house and drive away."

"I mean in the last few minutes."

"No. Why?"

"Wetzel's dead."

Ray's head jerked. "When did this happen?"

"You tell me!"

They put Ray Spensor under a lamp at the Sheriff's station and kept him there for nearly an hour. When it was over, Mark Storm came out of the interrogation room with a perplexed look on his face, hands stuffed in his pants pockets.

"That guy is either too smart or too dumb," the

deputy muttered. "I don't know which."

"Wouldn't he cooperate?" I asked.

"Sure. We couldn't shut him up. He told us everything. How he walked outside for some fresh air, how he bedded down in your back seat for a nap, how the sounds of people leaving woke him. He swears he never went near the house after he left."

"What was he doing in the garage?"

"He claims he was looking for a powder room."

"In the dark?"

Mark shrugged. "He says he couldn't find the light switch."

"I can believe that. It was pitch black." I lowered into a chair near Mark's desk and pursed my lips. "What I can't understand is why he didn't see or hear someone running down that walkway.

"He heard you," the deputy said, pushing a cigarette in his mouth.

"That's what I mean, Mark. I was trying to be as quiet as possible and yet he heard me. Why wouldn't he hear someone who was obviously in a big hurry?"

"Maybe our knife-wielding intruder went up over that embankment at the rear of the house."

"Too high. The wall's at least ten feet. He'd had to have gone out the walkway. That's what makes me wonder about Spensor."

Mark hitched up his pants. "You can't hang a man for not being observant, Honey. What about this Tunny dame?"

"She was in the living room with me when we heard

Wetzel cry out. He'd gone into his bedroom to get something he wanted to show me. I never found out what that was."

"What about the other guests?"

"I'd guess there were about thirty. More men than women. Probably a bunch of minor lights in the Hollywood firmament."

He made a note on his scratch pad. "I'll see if I can't check them out."

"What about Fred Sims?" I asked.

The deputy cocked his head at me and said, "I couldn't locate him. When I got up to Meadow Falls he'd already blown."

"Where, Mark?"

"Nobody knew. Incidentally, I checked those machines under the temple. They'd been disassembled."

I nodded. "We're batting a thousand all the way around."

"Yeah. But don't worry. I've got plans for Tunny."

"And Fred?"

"The jury's still out." He shook his head. "Get off my back, Honey! Fred's my best friend."

"Toy Tunny says Fred was intimately acquainted with Angela Scali."

Mark spun around, eyes glaring. "So what? Fred's a newspaper man. Don't you imagine he knows a lot of film personalities?"

"Sure," I said simply.

"Then take your cockeyed theories someplace else, will you?" he blared. "I'm sick of them!"

"Come on, Mark—"

"Come on, nothing!" He fixed a hard gaze on me. "You're always picking somebody's guts, aren't you, Honey? I'm surprised when your father wound up in that gutter you didn't blame Fred for killing him. He was the first one on the scene, wasn't he?"

"Yes," I said faintly.

He straightened, towering over me, glaring angrily. "Lay off Fred. In fact, take my advice and lay off this whole case before you get hurt!"

"I'm already hurt, Lieutenant," I said, crossing to his office door.

I walked out to the parking lot and climbed into my car. The clock on the dash indicated it was nearly three, but as far as I was concerned the night was still young.

I drove back to Box Canyon and up the steep road to Sol Wetzel's place again. The garage door was closed now and the house dark. The wind had died and stars blinked in the inky sky.

When deputies from the Sheriff's office checked Wetzel's bedroom they had looked for the obvious: fingerprints, shoe impressions, signs of a scuffle. They had not been aware of Wetzel's plan to show me something. I was certain that whatever it was, the object or objects had some bearing on the case.

I parked in the driveway and removed my .22 from its garter holster, then proceeded along the dark walkway to the bedroom door. It was locked. I continued on into the circular patio to a set of French doors. They were secured also, but I changed that with a quick rap of my revolver's butt against a pane of glass. The window splintered, leaving a hole wide enough for me to reach inside and release the latch. The doors opened into a small dining area, off the kitchen.

Once inside, I stiffened at the sound of a clock chiming somewhere in the house. The bell tolled three times and stopped. I moved around a table and chairs to the living room where I'd stood with Toy Tunny hours earlier.

Suddenly I got the feeling I was not alone in the house. I flattened against a wall listening, my gun hand lifted in readiness. A clock ticked on the fireplace mantel. Crickets drummed ceaselessly outside.

Finally I continued on into Wetzel's bedroom and switched on a desk lamp. The floor was still covered with papers, crumpled rugs and books which had fallen when the wind had blown them from a shelf. The bed had been torn apart by investigating deputies. Bloody sheets and blankets had been removed, leaving only a darkly stained mattress. I surveyed the room. Beside the desk and bed there was an old bureau in one corner and a clothes hamper. Next to this was a closet. The door stood open, revealing neatly hung suits and sports clothes and another bureau built inside the closet. I crossed quietly, keeping my ears tuned to any sounds that might emanate from other parts of the house. The closet bureau produced nothing but stacks of socks, undershorts, ties and white shirts. I checked the rear of each drawer carefully for any sign of papers or photographs.

Then I returned to the desk, noting the tape recorder

had been moved to allow a fingerprint expert to work. The deputies had placed the machine on top of the clothes hamper, but I noticed its long cord had not been disconnected from the wall socket. I started to lift the recorder down from the hamper when I realized the metal sides were warm. I examined the knobs. The one indicating volume was turned up to almost full. Both plastic reels were missing. I looked around for the one which had been knocked to the floor by the wind, but couldn't see it in the tangle of papers and books.

I froze again. Something rattled lightly in the living room. I placed the recorder back on the hamper and tiptoed to the desk lamp, flicking it off.

Certain sounds are hard to distinguish. This wasn't. The rhythmic thump of a cane striking a hard surface drifted in the darkness, drawing nearer, a leg dragging slightly. A huge shadow loomed in the door, then stopped.

"I know you're here," a voice said. "So don't pretend."

With my free hand I switched on the desk lamp again. Standing in the doorway, his head bent slightly, a cane gripped in his raw-boned fingers, was Thor Tunny.

And, of all things, he was fully clothed.

TWELVE

The huge, seven-foot cult leader didn't even wince at the sight of my revolver. He limped into the room slowly, head still bent, right hand gripping the cane. He was dressed in a brown business suit and a grey hat that slanted low on his forehead.

I waved the gun abruptly. "That's near enough, Mr. Tunny."

He glowered at me from under the hat, but didn't stop. "You'd be a fool to pull that trigger, Miss West."

"I'd be a bigger fool if I didn't," I said, index finger tightening. "Take my advice."

He made a quick move, sliding his cane on the floor, and hunched down on Wetzel's stained mattress, groaning softly. "All right. I've had enough exercise for the moment. Besides, my leg hurts."

"I thought it was your head that was in bad shape, Mr. Tunny."

He removed his hat, revealing a bandage. "That, too.

You did a thorough job, Miss West. Remind me to repay you sometime."

My gaze shifted to the door. "Who's with you?"

"No one," he said simply. "I drove up alone."

"I didn't hear your car."

He glanced around the room. "Perhaps your mind was further occupied. Apparently you've been busy. Did you find them?"

"Find what?"

He laughed oddly. "You're a poor detective, Miss West. You don't expect me to furnish your clues, do you?"

"I don't expect you to furnish anything, Mr. Tunny, except some answers to some questions. Like what are you doing here?"

He grinned cockily. "This is my house. Don't I have the right to be in my own place?"

"Don't be smart. You know Sol Wetzel's dead."

"Of course. Toy called me. Most unfortunate accident. Especially since for the second time such a thing occurs on my property."

"You own this house, is that it?"

"You are becoming more accurate by the second, Miss West. Bravo!" He applauded lightly, eyes scanning me. "And I might add, you are becoming more beautiful by the hour. Lissome legs, nicely tapered hips, good—"

"You can cut the geographical survey, Mr. Tunny."

He laced his fingers together, cracking their brittle joints. "Despite your uninhibited show of physical violence, Miss West, I find you extremely engaging. Too bad you chose such an unfortunate field of endeavor."

"Listen, Mr. Tin God," I countered. "I got a long look at your chamber of horrors. You talk about physical violence. I had a 22-year-old client who took one of your joy rides. She hasn't been able to talk straight since."

He shook his head, lips puckering. "You must be mistaken. My society is one of puritanical absolution. We frown on the sensual qualities."

I poked the gun under his nose. "Well start frowning at this."

Tunny nibbled at a fingernail for an instant, then said, "What is it that you wish?"

"What was your connection with Sol Wetzel?"

"I was his landlord."

"And?"

"That's all."

I pushed the gun against his forehead.

He swallowed deeply. "We—we were business partners."

"Keep talking."

"Sol had a—a financial interest in the camp."

"How big?"

Tunny winced. "Two-thirds."

"Where'd he get that kind of money?"

"I don't know."

"You lie!"

He stared up at the gleaming muzzle. "All right. He received it from Angela Scali."

"You mean he took it, don't you?"

"No. She gave him nearly everything she had. It was a bargain between them."

"What kind of a bargain?"

"She—Angela wanted out of the motion picture business. But she had an iron-clad contract with the studio. There was only one thing she could do. Disappear."

"That doesn't make sense," I said. "She could have bought her way out."

"She couldn't," Tunny protested. "She wanted to live at Meadow Falls. Angela and Wetzel both knew she'd never be free of publicity if she did it in the open. They had to go undercover."

"That still doesn't add up."

He shot pleading eyes in my direction. "The studio would have sued her for every cent she owned. It was either a case of disappear, or pay and be persecuted by the press. You know an Academy Award winner can't just step out because she wants to. Angela had too many obligations. To the American public, to newspapers and magazines and to her studio."

I lowered the revolver slowly. "Okay. How'd you figure in this?"

He gripped his sunburnt forehead with his hands as if trying to ward off any more thrusts of the gun barrel.

"I—I was ready to go under," he stammered. "There just weren't enough contributions, and too many mouths to feed. Their investment put us back on our feet."

"Are you sure this wasn't a deal cooked up by you and Wetzel alone?"

"No! I swear to you! It was all her idea. Wetzel was afraid from the very beginning."

"What was he afraid of?"

"That someone at the camp would talk. Or that Fred Sims would break his promise and print a story."

I straightened. "You knew Fred Sims then. You were pretending when we came into the temple yesterday."

"Of course. Fred was an old friend of the Angel's. In fact, he helped effect her escape the night of the awards at the Pantages Theatre."

I suddenly had the feeling he was feeding me. That he'd come here for that purpose.

"Let's go back to the beginning, Mr. T. Back twenty-four hours, to Rip Spensor. Why did his death bother you so much?"

Tunny cracked his knuckles, grimacing. "Angela disappeared early that same afternoon. She and Spensor had had a love affair during the summer. He'd been sworn to secrecy, but when I heard the report of his death over the radio I knew we were in trouble."

"Did you suspect Angela?"

"I didn't know whom to suspect. I only knew that with her gone and Spensor dead, we were sitting on a Mount Vesuvius."

"How did you get my name?"

"I called Fred Sims. He suggested I send somebody after you. So I sent Adam."

"Keep going."

"Well, the next thing I knew Adam returned empty-handed. He told me some crazy story about having a run-in with the Long Beach police. I was nearly frantic. I called a meeting of the congregation—"

"And that's when Fred and I came in, right?"

"Yes. I didn't know then that Toy and Ray Spensor had found Angela in your apartment. Or that—that Angela was dead."

"That just about brings us up to the present, doesn't it, Mr. T.? Except for a few minor hours, including those I spent trying to escape from your sex trap."

"I—I assure you, Miss West, that was all a grave mistake brought about by Fred's insistence that you be detained."

"Fred's insistence?"

"Yes," Tunny said, wiping his mouth. "He argued that your life was in danger. That you'd be better off if we created some nonsensical reason for your staying at Meadow Falls."

"It was nonsensical all right, Mr. Tunny. If you had tried that playground bit on me, sooner or later I'd have torn the place apart.

He tried to rise, but my gun held him in his place. "That was a pretense, Miss West. Don't you understand? Fred told us to suspect anybody, including Ray Spensor. When we found Spensor with you we only assumed—"

"You assumed wrong, Mr. T. Ray was trying to do anything but kill me. You're still reaching."

"I'm telling you the truth."

"And what's the truth about your daughter? What was her connection with Sol Wetzel?"

He shook his head dismally. "They were friends. What more can I say?"

"You could say they were a couple of perverted pals. That knife games to them were like a rubber of bridge to Charles Goren."

"I don't understand my daughter," Tunny said, "so I don't attempt to analyze her or her friends."

"Bully for you. Well analyze this then, Mr. Sun God. Toy and Ray Spensor spirited Angela Scali away from my apartment. They, above anyone else, knew she was back at camp. Now who else possibly could have known?"

"Adam, I suppose. He acted very strangely that morning."

"Who else?"

"Fred Sims."

My fist slammed on the desk. "Why do you keep bringing up his name. You know very well Fred was with me. How could he possibly have known?"

Tunny exhaled loudly, drumming his cane on the floor. "Miss West, you remind me of a lost soul wandering in the dark. Don't you know who Fred Sims really is?"

"Sure," I said, thinking about the ribbon I'd found. "He's a nice friendly guy who got half a leg blown off and has half a Congressional Medal of Honor to show for it. Now you tell me."

He laughed grimly, rising halfway on his injured leg and shifting his cane under him. "Don't you know why he kept the secret?"

"I've been wondering," I said. "Fred usually keeps only one secret and that's where he's hidden the next bottle."

"Angela met him during the war," Tunny said.

"So?"

"He saved her life. She was just a dark-haired kid hiding in a shell hole. Mother and father blown to bits.

Fred carried her across a mine field to safety. Angela never forgot that."

"I can understand why," I said. "But that was par for the course for Fred Sims. He turned Bastogne into a Roman holiday for the Allies."

"I've heard that story," Tunny said, staring at me blankly. "Have you heard this one?"

"Which one?"

"Fred and Angela." His eyes gleamed when he said the words. "They were married in a small church outside Rome. Fifteen years ago."

THIRTEEN

The roof might have fallen in on me. I hunched forward, lowered my revolver and exhaled. The room spun around and then straightened.

"You—you have proof?" I demanded.

"Fred showed me the paper when he brought Angela to the camp. I accepted the document for what it was worth."

My teeth clamped tight. "And it was worth plenty to you, wasn't it, Mr. T? Another sucker. Another big bankroll."

"Despite what you imagine, Miss West," he countered, "the camp is a legitimate operation. We've accepted donations, yes, but always openly."

"How open was Angela Scali?"

"She was the exception. I only did that, as I told you, because of extreme financial circumstances. If need be, I'll testify to that fact."

"And will you testify to the machines beneath your temple?"

His forehead ridged. "Those were Toy's idea. I must admit they were crude and perverse. They did serve one purpose."

"And what's that?" I said. "Ruining a dozen or more nice young girls?"

"No," he said flatly. "Unfortunately there are some people who enjoyed them. In every society there are those few."

"Yourself included?"

"They've been junked, Miss West. And that ends that. So why pursue the matter?"

I didn't answer. The revelation of Fred and Angela's marriage in Italy kept ramming through my brain. It seemed utterly impossible that Fred could keep such a secret all these years. Worse was the fact that he'd been in on the Rip Spensor-Angela Scali case from the very start and yet never said anything. Never tipped his hand. I glowered at Tunny's cane.

"Where'd you get that stick?" I demanded, anger welling hotly inside me.

"This? I've had it for years. Developed a bad case of gout when I first opened Meadow Falls. Why?"

"Where was it yesterday?"

"In my office at the camp."

"Did anybody borrow it?"

"I don't believe so. What are you getting at, Miss West?"

"Who has access to your office besides yourself?"

"Several people. All my directors have keys."

"Adam Jason?"

"Yes. Even Ray Spensor has a key, I believe. In fact, he makes a hobby of collecting keys. I was going to change the lock after he left my organization, but I don't keep my valuables there so I didn't bother."

"Where does Ray Spensor live?"

Tunny scratched his neck thoughtfully. "I understand he's been sharing a house with his cousin, Rip. Out near a hundred and eighty-something and Figueroa."

I started for the door, then fixed my eyes on Tunny again. "When you came in you asked me if I'd found them. Now I'm asking you for the last time, what were you referring to?"

He shrugged complacently. "It was just a figure of speech, dear lady. Knowing you, I wouldn't imagine you were here speculating over the desirability of an abruptly vacant rental."

I gestured at the tape recording machine. "Earlier, before Wetzel was murdered, there were two reels of tape on that machine. One of them fell on the floor. Now both are missing. I don't believe they were removed by the investigating deputies. Could they be the *them* you were referring to?"

He smiled knowingly. "Miss West, I hired you, but you refused to work for me. Now you are trying to enlist my aid. I will not be a party to your private housebreaking. Nor will I tolerate your vicious tactics. I'm filing suit against you for assault and battery, for breaking and entering, for illegal use of firearms against an unarmed citizen, for—"

"Save your breath, Mr. Tunny," I interrupted harshly.

"When the D.A. finishes with you and your sex camp, the only suit you'll be filing is the one on your back in moth balls. Get up!"

His face colored. "Don't threaten me, Miss West. I know my rights."

"Get up!"

Tunny lifted himself slowly, leaning heavily on his cane.

"Move to the other side of the room," I directed.

He followed my order hesitantly, hands trembling. I bent down beside the bed and peered under the box springs. Papers and books were scattered underneath where they'd blown or been kicked earlier. Then my eyes caught the glint of a plastic reel, almost covered by a manila folder against the wall. I flattened on my stomach and crawled under until I had the spool in my fingers, then I slithered out and stood up.

"Well," I said, glancing at Tunny. "Here's one of the reels. Now if I can find an empty one we'll hear how she plays."

He didn't appear concerned over my discovery, but a muscle in his sunburnt face twitched as I began searching through some of the desk drawers.

"You have no right to do this, Miss West," he protested. "You could be arrested."

"I'll see to it we share the same cell, Mr. T. and maybe we'll have a game of Scrabble. The kind where every word spells *murder*."

He shuddered. I found an empty spool in a bottom drawer, fitted both reels to the tape recorder and hooked them together. Then I pushed the PLAY button.

For five minutes we stood stiffly in our places listening to absolute silence, except for the creak of the spools as they turned. Several times I fumbled with different knobs, including the volume control, but they didn't change the end result. When the tape had run out, Tunny laughed.

"Thank you, Miss West, for a few minutes of quiet, at any rate," he said glibly. "Now are you satisfied to vacate my property peacefully?"

I removed the half-filled reel and spun it through my fingers thoughtfully. Two spools. One missing. I guessed I'd found the half which had not yet passed through the recording channel.

I tossed the reel on the desk and nodded. "You win this trip, Mr. T. But we'll meet again for the rubber match, don't worry."

I was halfway through the outside door when I turned back and picked up the tape. "I think I'll keep this as a memento of the occasion."

"No!" he protested, moving toward me.

"I thought you were going to say that. There are two sides to these things. Perhaps I'll have better success reversing the reel. Good night, Mr. Tunny. Pleasant dreams."

I closed the door behind me and moved down the walkway. The sky was the color of dirty dishwater and new rain pelted down on my face. Tunny's car was parked next to mine. I checked for hidden occupants, then climbed inside my own convertible. There were no uninvited passengers there either, hairy or otherwise. I waited for a minute to see if Tunny might come out of the house, but he didn't. He was shrewd and calculating and knew more than he'd told me. That was what bothered me most. He'd said just enough to steer me straight toward Fred Sims, Ray Spensor and Adam Jason. I thought I'd pick on Spensor first. His disappearing acts were getting to be as famous as Houdini's, if not as enchanting. His gate stunt had been fairly understandable. Tunny's strong-arm tactics hurt. His vanishing act at Wetzel's had not made sense. Neither had his explanation to Mark Storm that he'd needed some fresh air. Ray's interest in the sensual side of life made his disappearance in the middle of Toy's naked contortions seem pretty contrived.

I drove down the mountain slowly, prepared for any sudden decrease in braking power, but I reached the bottom without any trouble. Charley April supplied me with Ray Spensor's correct address over the auto phone. He growled about the interruption, claiming this was his only hour of good sleep and then cautioned me to be careful.

It was four-thirty by the time I reached the squat frame house off a Hundred and eighty-second and Figueroa. The asphalt road in front was criss-crossed with ugly deep grooves apparently dug by the road-grading equipment which came to retrieve Rip Spensor's mangled body after he'd been flattened by the steam roller. I couldn't help the shiver that raced up my back as I climbed from the car. Rip had been such a nice guy.

Gentle. Sweet. This seemed a tragic way to die.

I moved to the front porch and rang the bell. After a moment, a light flicked on and footsteps banged inside the house.

Ray Spensor appeared in a splash of porch light, rubbing his eyelids, a robe drawn around his husky shoulders.

"Honey," he said, gaping at me through the screen. "What in hell are you doing here?"

"Accepting a long standing invitation extended by your cousin," I said, brushing through some gnarled wet strands of hair. "Aren't you going to invite me into your parlor?"

"You're drenched," he said, opening the screen. "Come on in. I'll fix a fire."

I entered the living room, shaking drops of water from my shoulders, scanning his unshaven face cautiously. "You wouldn't have a cup of coffee, would you?"

"I've got better than that," he said. "How about a spot of brandy? You look beat."

"I am," I agreed quickly. "I haven't slept in over twenty-four hours, except for that brief stretch of night-night Angela Scali tapped into my head. How are you fixed for beds?"

He flicked a puzzled grin at me and nodded. "Loaded." He extended his arms. "The joint's yours. If you can disregard a sink full of dirty dishes, a couple of bedrooms with messed up sheets and laundry, and a mighty delirious football player named Spensor."

He led me into the kitchen where the sink was more

than filled. It was bulging with dishes, pots and pans. He poured two shots of brandy and got me a towel. That's when I spotted the cane hanging on a rack on the back porch.

"Who belongs to that?" I asked, rubbing my face with the cloth.

Ray glanced at the cane blankly. "Oh, that. Rip wrecked his knee last year in one of the Colt games. He hobbled around on that thing for weeks."

I lifted the cane from the rack and examined its tip. The rubber cap was missing. There was dried mud the lower end of the shaft.

"Looks like it's been used recently," I said. "You get hurt in that Forty-niner game?"

His brows knitted as he studied the crust of dried mud. "No. That's funny. I wonder if—"

"What?" I demanded.

He stared at me tautly. "I wonder if Rip was faking about the play the week before in the Bear game. He was pretty shook up on the last run from scrimmage. I thought sure he'd re-injured his leg."

"Did he say he had?"

"No, but Rip was funny that way. He didn't like to miss a game. He was limping in that 49'er game, the night he was killed."

"Didn't the coach say anything?"

"Sure, he said plenty, but Rip was running fairly well so he left him in," Ray stroked his forehead with the flat of his hand. "That could explain why he didn't get out of the way of that steam roller."

"You mean he might have tried to run, but his leg gave out on him?"

"That's right." He scrutinized the cane. "I'm glad you noticed this, Honey. It explains a lot."

"Does it, Ray?" I studied his face carefully.

"Sure. Ask yourself why a man as fast as Rip could be cut down by a machine as slow and lumbering as a steam roller. A leg injury, that's the only answer."

"Ray, are you certain you didn't know about his injury? Somebody must have known."

His face flushed angrily. "Of course I didn't. I just told you I wondered, that's all."

"Okay," I said. "Let's drink to that."

"No," he countered slyly. "Let's drink to you, Honey. To you and your devious ways. Why don't you tell the truth? You didn't come here for a cup of coffee or a free bed. You've got wheels turning. Confess."

"All right," I said. "I just ran into a man named Tunny who says you're quite a collector of keys. The set belonging to the steam roller turned up missing after Rip was murdered. Who collected them?"

"How should I know?" he slammed, sipping at his brandy. "I wasn't even here when it all happened."

"Where were you, Ray?"

"At a little bar on Forty-eighth. Having a sandwich."

"Any witnesses?"

"I went all through this with your friend Lieutenant Storm at least a dozen times. The waitress doesn't remember me."

"Why not?"

"She went off-duty shortly after I arrived. Her mind must have been preoccupied."

I shook my head, wiping more beads of water into the towel. "That sounds awfully thin, Ray."

"I know it does," he said. "But what am I supposed to do, invent witnesses? Pull them out of my hat? I'm no Houdini."

"Funny you should say that," I said. "I was likening you to him earlier. You do pull some awfully neat tricks. Like Wetzel's house. You went up in a puff of smoke."

"I told Storm, I got sick to my stomach. And that's exactly what happened."

"Why didn't you tell me before you left?"

"Because," he said evenly, "I was too sick to say anything."

"How long have you been home?" I asked.

He stuck his big hands in the pockets of his robe and exhaled. "Come on, Honey. Drop the female wolfdog bit and relax. I've been interrogated up to here. And the answer is still the same. No."

"No, what?"

"No, I had nothing to do with Sol Wetzel's murder—or Angela Scali's—or—"

He stopped as he noticed my eyes fixed on a large coffee can sitting on the corner of the sink. The brand name didn't interest me, but the jagged holes cut in the top did. I picked up the container and examined it closely.

"What's this?" I asked.

Ray removed his hands from his pockets and jiggled them nervously. "The—the coffee I offered you."

"You must have been in a terrible hurry to open the can."

I shook the container. Something rattled inside.

"That—that's at least a month old," he said, lifting down a jar of instant from the cupboard. "This is what I've been drinking."

Before he could stop me I jerked open the lid and peered inside. His face paled. So did mine. I dropped the can, as a huge spider flipped out on the floor, its hairy legs still in death.

"I notice you drink your coffee black, Ray," I said. "Okay, start brewing."

"Honey, you don't understand," he protested, staring at the twisted spider.

"What is there to understand, Ray? Do you can and sell these by the dozen? They must be quite a delicacy."

"I—"

I extracted my revolver from beneath my skirt and leveled it at him. "You can talk plainer than that. Some kindly gentleman deposited half a dozen of these in my car night before last. They nearly had me in stitches."

"Honey," he pleaded, "you won't believe this, but—but that thing belonged to Rip. He collected spiders. Especially mygales. They're a variety of tarantula. It was a hobby with him."

"Rip was already dead when this incident occurred, Ray. Try a disappearing act, it's more your specialty. That's what my friend did after he dumped his merchandise in my convertible."

"I—I had nothing to do with that."

"Somebody did. Don't tell me you've got the same alibi. That you were in that bar on Forty-eighth."

He wiped at his face clumsily. "Why would I want to hurt you, Honey?"

"You have the floor, Mr. Spensor. You tell me."

"I told you Rip collected spiders. He has a whole cage full of those things buried in the ground alive."

"Where?"

"Out in back."

"Show me," I said, waving the revolver at the rear door.

I watched him carefully as he took a flashlight from a drawer. Then he led the way out into the dark rainy night, through a muddy yard to a fence and a small covered arbor.

He bent down in one corner and removed a wooden cover from a hole in the ground. In the flashlight's glare I could see a wire cage beneath. Rain dripped from the slats above us.

I stood back as he examined the cage, then he got to his feet slowly, face contorted.

"They—they're gone," he said emptily.

"And so are you, pal," I added. "Only this time it isn't going to be out the nearest exit—or to a bar on Forty-eighth. It's going to be behind some bars at the Sheriff's station."

FOURTEEN

"Honey!" Ray protested, rain drenching down on his face. "I—I'm in love with you!"

"So was Othello in love with Desdemona before he strangled her. Back to the house!"

Hands swinging numbly at his sides, Ray walked across the yard, not even bothering to light the way. When he reached the door his numbness suddenly faded. He whipped the panel back into my face, knocking me from the porch. I fell into a narrow ditch half-filled with water and mud, the revolver slipping from my grasp.

By the time I found the gun and crawled to my feet, he was long gone, racing wildly across a vacant lot, legs flying. He vanished in the darkness and rain. I started after him, reaching the middle of the next lot before I decided to give up the search. Beyond was a wide open stretch of trees and scattered houses. And miles of no man's land. He'd be hard to find even with a pack of dogs. I knew I didn't really want Ray Spensor anyway.

Not now. He was doing exactly what I'd hoped he would do. Disappear. For good.

At my apartment in Alamitos Bay I found the guy I was really looking for. He sat in my living room, legs cocked up on an ottoman snoring peacefully. I nudged him gently. His eyelids fluttered open and he grinned knowingly.

"Hello, Honey," he said, stretching. "Your back door lock was broken, so I took the liberty of coming in out of the rain. You look like you've been playing with mud pies."

"Hello, Adam," I said. "I thought you were dead."

"You mean now or earlier? Those goons of Tunny's weren't very nice."

He indicated a bruise on the side of his face.

"Too bad, Adam," I said, edging my voice with sarcasm. "You seem to be everybody's fall guy, don't you? Why not join my club?"

He was dressed in a T-shirt and slacks that were still wet from the weather. "What club's that?"

"Fall Guys, Incorporated. I'm chief mucka-muck. The entrance examinations are easy. One low kick or a bum steer within the past few days, fully certified, and you're in."

"Honey, you're pulling my leg."

I smiled. "That's what you think."

He suddenly reached for me hungrily, but I drew back from his outstretched hands.

"Honey!" he sighed.

"Take it easy, pal. You've left your motor running. Excuse me while I shower."

I left him trembling and red-faced, locked myself inside the bedroom and stripped off my clothes. The warmth of the shower was so luxurious, I felt like singing as the water gushed over me. There were only two problems remaining. One was Adam Jason. I had a feeling he would be easy to handle. I didn't know then what I learned five minutes later. If I had I'd doubtlessly have remained behind the locked door.

I came out in a tailored blue robe, my hair pulled up in a top knot, and wearing no makeup. The look on Adam's face told me the wrap-around robe was a big mistake. A tailored tent would have been safer. He gaped at me open-mouthed and then poured us each a martini from a frosted pitcher.

"Honey, you—you're ravishing," Adam said, toasting my outfit.

I sipped at my martini. "I think you've already had enough to drink, Adam."

He was extremely handsome and he knew it. He brushed back a few damp locks of black hair and said, "You like me, don't you?"

"I already told you I did. At my office." The martini was beginning to feel as powerful as a steam roller on a dark road. I shook my head. "What did you put in this thing?"

"Ten jiggers of gin and an olive," he said. "You like?"

"After not eating or sleeping for two days, I'll have to admit it's delicious. It'll probably make me fat." He put a cigarette between his lips and offered me one. He was really feeling his oats. The time had come, I thought, to lower the boom. But suddenly I didn't feel like dangling him on a string. He was nice, and the evening was still young. Even if it was almost dawn. I laughed.

"I'll never forget you standing in my office wearing nothing but my skirt and sweater. Or the look on your face when the police pulled up in that squad car." I swallowed some more of my drink and the burning sensation warmed me to the toes.

"The joke was on them, wasn't it, Honey?"

"Yeah. Hey, you do make an excellent martini."

He refilled my glass. That's when I suddenly realized the joke was on me. The level of his glass was still high. I reeled back, flinging my drink to the floor.

"You—you put something in that," I said.

"I was wondering when you were going to wake up—or rather go to sleep." His face began to blur.

"Why, Adam?"

He moved around the bar toward me. "Honey, don't you realize what you've been doing?"

"What?" I stumbled over a stool, got up, fell again. "Adam, I didn't really think—"

"That's the trouble with you, Honey. You didn't really think." He sounded different now. His voice was deep and resonant "Neither did the rest of them, including Thor Tunny. You're right. They thought I was a fall guy, but I wasn't. I never have been."

"You—you know about Sol Wetzel?"

"And Fred Sims—and Ray Spensor. I know everything. I was the guy everybody counted out. But they didn't realize."

My senses reeled and I groped for the couch, pulling

myself up to a sitting position. "You—you said you played football with Rip at Notre Dame. I—I believed you."

"It was a lie, Honey. I'm sorry. I lied to you about several things, including where I was the night Rip was murdered."

"You—you mean—you—" I slumped over sideways, eyes staring up at his contorted face as he advanced toward me.

"I'm the one who put the tarantulas in your car, Honey." His voice dropped apologetically. "I had to."

"Why?"

He knelt beside me. "You were in the way. Don't you understand? You were in the way! Why did you ever do it?"

"Do what?" I asked weakly, hardly able to keep my eyes focused on his mouth.

"Get mixed up with Rip Spensor. If you hadn't, this never would have happened, Honey. You would have continued the way you are. Beautiful, vibrant, alive."

"Adam—Adam, you're not going to kill me?"

His voice broke. "Yes."

"I—I still don't understand," I forced, stammering, breath high in my throat. "You don't fit the pattern. You had no motive."

"I've got the biggest motive in the world, Honey."

"Not—not money?"

"No," he said, leaning over me. "Don't talk anymore, please."

"Hate?"

"Leave me be, Honey," he mumbled, reaching for my throat.

"You—you couldn't have hated them, Adam!"

"I hate everybody, do you understand? Everybody! They never leave me alone. Not for a minute."

My eyes closed, my head filled with a reddish glow. "Adam, don't do it!"

"I've got to, Honey," his voice drifted. "I have to. I'm sorry."

The lid closed in on me. I drifted for an instant on a red cloud that bubbled and rolled. Then I dropped through a thousand miles of space filled with nothing but darkness. When I hit bottom I landed so hard it seemed as if all my clothes were torn from me. I screamed. Then a wave of cool light bathed over me and I blinked and died.

When the light came again I wasn't sure. But it felt warm and good on my face. I opened my eyes, expecting to see a long infinite length of billowing clouds, but a drab green ceiling cut sharply into view.

I tried to straighten. A weight was heavy on my arms and legs and chest. I couldn't move. Pushing against it seemed futile until I shifted sideways. Then it fell beside me with a dull thump. I sat up and shook my head.

Blinking from bright sunshine that blazed in from a window across the room, I looked around dazedly. I was sitting on the floor of my living room. A pitcher of martinis was still perched on the bar across from me. So was a glass. Slowly I let my eyes drift to my side. A man lay twisted there. His eyes were open and filmed from death. I crawled to my feet, staggered to the bar and poured a martini from the pitcher. Then, remembering what had happened, I pitched the glass across the room.

It seemed nonsensical, but there he was.

I turned slowly and stared down at him.

He'd been lying on my chest when I came awake. He'd been there a long time. Perhaps for hours. I glanced at the clock over my range. It was almost twelve noon.

FIFTEEN

Three hours later, Sheriff's deputies had chalked, sprayed and dusted my apartment.

Mark Storm finally cornered me alone in the bedroom, a scowl on his big face. "You okay?" he asked bluntly.

"I think so," I said.

The deputy slumped into a chair in the corner and regarded me tautly. "You asked for this, Honey."

"I asked for only one thing, Lieutenant. A logical suspect. Looks like I came up with one."

"He's too dead to tell," Mark said, rubbing his forehead grimly. "He looks like he bit into a sour lemon."

"Poison?"

"Yep."

I shook my head. "I guess I'm lucky he didn't give me some of the same stuff."

"We found a bottle in his wallet pocket," Mark said. "It's colorless. Hector says it may be strychnine."

"You believe he took it himself?"

"How else?"

I groaned. "He admitted putting those spiders in my car."

"Nice guy," Mark said. "Of course, you entertain only the best."

"I wasn't entertaining."

"What were you doing?" he demanded. "I don't see a Scrabble board out there."

"Okay," I admitted. "I was trying to prove something, but my plan flopped."

"Yeah, right in the middle of the living room floor!"

Mark removed a crumpled piece of paper from his coat pocket and handed it to me. "Ever see this before?"

Carefully scrawled on the face of the paper were these words: I confess to the murders of Rip Spensor, Angela Scali and Sol Wetzel. The note was signed *Adam Jason*.

"Poor Adam," I said, groaning softly. "He was a pretty mixed-up guy."

"So you told me," the deputy said, sitting on the edge of the bed. "What do you think went wrong with his plan to shorten your life span?"

"I have no idea." I could tell Mark was skeptical of the note. He had that knowing look he always gets when he thinks he knows something nobody else does.

"Well," he sighed, after a moment. "I guess this wraps it up. We'll probably never know why he killed them. That secret died with him."

"That's right," I said idly, tracing my fingers along

the edge of the blanket. "I guess you won't need me any more, will you?"

"No." He got to his feet and tucked the note into his pocket. "You'd better get some rest. I'll call you tomorrow. I will need your signed statement."

"Sure, Lieutenant."'

He crossed to the door, then paused. "You—you do believe he wrote this note, don't you?"

"Of course," I said. "Who else could have written it?"

"Nobody," he said with gruff authority. "We checked against other handwriting in his wallet. I just wanted to be sure you were convinced."

"I'm convinced," I answered simply, trying to hide a smile that flicked across my mouth. I started to tell him about Fred and Angela, then decided against it. He'd said the case was closed. Besides he'd asked me not to mention Fred again. My conscience was clear.

Five minutes later Mark and his deputies had cleared out of my living room leaving only chalk marks on the hardwood floor where Adam's body had landed after I sat up. I showered again, slipped into a sweater and skirt and dialed the *Press-Telegram* newspaper office. They transferred me to Editorial.

Fred Sims sounded half loaded when he finally came on the line. "Well if it isn't the maid of Asphalt Lane," he said sharply. "I understand you came out on the hard end again. Congratulations."

"I want to talk to you, Fred."

"Never a time like the present," he said thickly. "I

was just on my way to a tangle of vines and heather down on the Pike where they serve the best waterballs in creation. Want to join me?"

"You mean the Jungle Room?"

"That's right. I plan to get completely crocked, so don't keep me waiting too long. I hate to drink alone unless it's mandatory."

"I'll be there in twenty minutes."

"Make it fifteen and the first round's on me."

"Okay," I said, meaningfully, "but the last round's going to be mine."

The sun was already low on a dark windy sea as I drove out Ocean Avenue to downtown Long Beach. Neon lights began to blink on shops and stores and going home traffic piled up in the streets. I parked in the lot opposite my office building and walked a half block before recalling the tape I'd picked up at Sol Wetzel's house. I retraced my steps quickly. The reel was gone from the front seat where I'd left it. I fumbled around on the floor, finally finding the spool lodged next to the heater. I contemplated leaving the tape in my office, then decided it was just as safe locked in my car.

Fred was waiting for me in the Jungle Room, his good leg curled under him on the stool, a drink clutched in his slender fingers.

He smiled grimly and said, "You're two drinks late."

"I was one drink early last night," I said, climbing onto a stool. "I suppose you got the word about Adam Jason."

"Several thousand words," Fred answered, shaking

his head drunkenly. "You would have thought the reporter from UPI was writing a book. It must have been jolly."

"It was unexpected, to say the least. Jason was not a suspect in my book."

Fred flicked his steel-grey eyes at me and laughed. "Who'd you have in mind?" He lifted his hand. "Before you answer, how about a drink? Something teeth-rattling."

"Why not?" I said. "My teeth have been doing nothing else but—for the past two days."

He ordered a round and said, "Honey, you know what your trouble is? Tension. You're a bundle of nerves. You need a vacation."

"Where would you suggest, Fred, Italy?"

His jaw tightened. "Sure. It's beautiful there this time of the year. Tall willowy trees. The wind blowing morning fresh off the Mediterranean. You'd love it."

"Of course, it's changed some since you were there," I said pointedly. "There aren't any more shell holes with dark-haired young girls hiding in them."

Fred removed his hat slowly and brushed at his thinning brown hair. "You have been getting around, haven't you?"

"A little. Level with me, Fred. Were you married to Angela Scali?"

He studied his glass for a long moment, then nodded. "That wasn't her name then, but I guess it'll do. Hollywood has an ugly way of changing most everything, doesn't it?"

"Did Angela change much?"

He hunched on the bar solemnly, eyes riveted on the mirror behind the bottles. "Fifteen years is a long time, Honey. She was skinny then. And frightened. So was I. The war was the big thing. The end of the road. There was no tomorrow."

"How old was she then, Fred?"

"Sixteen. She had a face like a madonna. And I was all of twenty-two. Two hands, two arms, two legs—" He stopped, quickly emptied his glass and stood up, grasping his cane. "Let's take a walk."

"I haven't touched my drink yet."

"Leave it. We'll come back."

"Will we, Fred?"

He grasped my arm. "You can bet on it. Come on."

We walked out into the glare of the Pike, its lights whirling, jiggling in the new darkness. The music from the merry-go-round blared in our ears. He led me to a bench near the roller coaster and pointed his stick at the shiny dark rails.

"See that thing, Honey. Every fifty-six seconds another one of those crazy-looking cars starts up over those tracks. Rain or shine. Kind of silly, isn't it?"

One of the cars careened around a curve, clanking violently.

"It's one way of making a living, Fred," I answered tautly. "How are you doing?"

He scratched his forehead. "As a star reporter I'm doing fine. I drink when I want to, write when I wish, sleep when I feel like it. The pay is good and I have no complaints. I wouldn't want to trade with you."

"Neither would I," I said, regarding his face intently. "How come you never brought Angela over to this country after the war?"

"Honey, you never bother with little questions, do you?"

"I learned that from you, Fred. You always told me to start at the top and work down. Were you worried about your leg?"

"Get off my back, Honey!" he slammed, rapping his cane on the pavement.

"Were you too pathetic, Fred, is that it? A guy with a stubbed-off leg who couldn't face the future?"

"I faced the future," he roared. "What do you want from me? Blood? Well, I left a gallon at Bastogne. So climb on your bicycle and go collect it!"

"Look at me, I'm weeping," I said harshly. "Too bad your Congressional didn't sprout five toes so you could have worn it on your stump instead of that artificial contraption."

He recoiled, tried to stand, then slumped on the bench heavily. "I taught you good, didn't I?" he said in his throat. "Never pull your punches. Always hit when they're down."

"You aren't down, Mr. Sims," I hurled. "You're just crawling. That's worse."

"Okay, so I didn't bring her here," he said lowly, staring up at the spindly-legged framework of rails and beams where a new car roared down. "Do you think I wanted her to see me like this?"

"You're no basket case, Fred."

"Neither was she. After a few years she did some acting with an Italian film company, then came a contract with a Hollywood studio. She arrived flashing a mink, a poodle and two very attractive knees. I was at the airport but she didn't even look at me."

"What'd you expect, a red-carpeted shell hole?"

"No!"

"You admitted fifteen years was a long time, Fred. Was it ever really a marriage?"

"No," he breathed lowly. "Even the Army didn't know about it. We found a priest secretly."

"So when she arrived here you went to the airport not as Fred Sims, husband and hero, but as Fred Sims reporter. Isn't that about it?"

"Yes. I didn't want her to know me. I was glad."

"Sure you were," I said. "But the feeling didn't last, did it?"

"No."

"You went after her, didn't you, Fred?"

"Yes," he managed grimly.

"Now she was big time."

"That wasn't the reason, Honey." His eyes sought mine and bored deeply. "Whatever you think, I was in love with Angela."

"Were you in love with her yesterday?"

"Yes!"

"Were you in love with her when you saw her dangling from that tree?"

He crushed his hands over his eyes. "Honey, don't do this to me!"

The roller coaster roared above us, booming on the thin rails, gnashing angrily.

"What did you do to yourself, Fred? That's what I want to know."

"Months ago I—I went to her," he whispered lowly. "I confessed who I was. She was living in a big apartment off Sunset Boulevard—with a swimming pool—and maids—and a butler. I'd been going there often, pretending interviews, making excuses that something had to be rewritten. I—I don't know why she took it the way she did."

"What'd she say, Fred? Thanks for the memory?"

"She—she called me a sick, crippled old man," he said faintly, staring off at the blinking, whirling lights of the Pike. "She laughed at me."

"I'm surprised," I said sarcastically. "I thought she might applaud. Especially when you showed her your Congressional."

"Stop it, Honey!"

"Stop what, Fred?" I drummed angrily. "Angela from dying? She was already dead when she came to the United States, wasn't she?"

"No!"

"You knew she was unhappy. You tried to help her, didn't you, Fred?"

"Yes!"

"You effected her escape from the Pantages Theatre. You took her to Meadow Falls."

"Yes," he groaned pitifully.

"Then what happened, Fred?"

"She—she forgot me," he said through clenched teeth. "She treated me again like she did at the beginning. She said she hated me!"

"Enough to make you want to murder her?"

"No!"

I groped inside his breast coat pocket. Before he jerked back I knew for certain his ribbon was not there. I produced the blood-stained emblem from my purse and held it up before his startled eyes.

"I found this in her shower stall, Fred."

He twisted awkwardly on the bench, clenching his hands. "Honey, I went to the camp yesterday morning. She wasn't in her apartment. So I took a walk up by the falls." His head dropped back, mouth open. "She—she was hanging from that tree. I—"

"Fred, you're going to need a good lawyer."

"Believe me, Honey. I didn't kill her. I must have gone out of my head. I remember reaching up for her, trying to lift her down. Then, everything went blank, until I found myself in her shower trying to wash off the blood."

"Then you drove to my apartment, didn't you?"

"Yes."

"You seemed perfectly sane when I saw you."

"I was, Honey," he broke, trying to talk above the rattle of the roller coaster above us. "I was sane the whole time, except—"

"Except when, Fred?"

He stiffened, drawing his cane up between us. "Let's take a ride on that thing. I've always watched, but never had courage enough to try it. Are you game, Honey?"

I peered up at the car sliding perilously along the rails and grimaced. "You haven't finished, Fred."

"I'll finish when we come down, Honey. I promise." He got up, shuffling his cane under him and produced some change from his pocket. "You're game, aren't you, Honey?"

"I guess so."

We started toward a runway into the ride where a woman sat inside a small booth counting money.

"This should be fun," Fred said, laying his change on the counter. "Like old times, huh, Honey?"

"Sure, Fred."

He lifted his cane under him as we walked toward a car poised below the girders and beams that made up the rickety old structure. He helped me inside and then climbed in, laughing drunkenly. "I remember the night your father was killed, Honey. You weren't much more than a kid then. I remember you kneeling in that gutter, weeping. I really felt sorry for you."

The car jerked forward, grinding around a sharp curve, starting up the steep incline that would hurtle us around the rails.

Fred thrust an arm around my shoulders and laughed. "You see how this works, Honey? They drag you to the top by means of a hook and a mechanical chain belt. Then you're on your own. The inertia built up from the first dip carries you all the way to the end. Fascinating, isn't it?"

The chain clanked beneath us, dragging the car toward the highest point of the spindly structure. Far below an empty car spun around a curve, flicking metallic sparks in the darkness.

"Fred, you might as well tell me," I said.

"Tell you what?"

"Why you came up to that cabin yesterday afternoon."

His eyes clung to the rails ahead of us. "What cabin?"

"The one on top of the mountain."

"Is that where I was?" he asked, not looking at me.

"What do you mean?"

"I told you there was a blank period after I found Angela. Another one occurred later that afternoon. I woke up near the falls, face down in the rain."

The car jerked on the tracks.

"Don't alibi, Fred."

"I'm not."

I unbuttoned my sweater, revealing broken skin above the V of my bra. "See this?"

He winced, sucking loudly on his teeth.

"A cane," I said, buttoning the garment up again. "I have another memento on my shoulder and one above my right knee."

"I—I don't understand," Fred stammered, shifting his eyes to the rails.

"I didn't think you would. Fred, where were you before this—this second blackout occurred?"

He shook his head dazedly. "I—I don't remember exactly. I believe I was in Thor Tunny's office. Toy wanted to talk to me—"

The car reached the top of the incline, lurched for an instant as the hook disengaged, and then pitched forward on the rails. The steel, dimly lit abyss below screamed toward us. The wind tore at our lungs. We swung into the first dip with such a grinding, heart-thumping roar that the beamed structure seemed to be breaking apart around us, flying past our heads, whirling.

I felt Fred's arms grip me in a wild frenzy, one hand smothering my eyes. I struggled, reeling sideways in the car as it banked around a steep turn, careening above the beach. He pushed me against the door of the car, snapping my head back, forcing me over the side.

"Fred!" I screamed. "Fred!"

"Honey!" his voice echoed above the din.

I felt my arms flailing, legs kicking wildly.

The car banked again into a steep dive.

SIXTEEN

Half out of the car, I rode the next turn screaming at the top of my lungs. The sound rattled above the gnashing metal, searing through the wood beams of the roller coaster ride, splitting up through the night.

"Fred!"

"You killed her, Honey!" he roared.

"No!"

"You killed Angela!"

The car swerved violently, throwing Fred against the opposite side. I caught my balance, swung an elbow into his face. Blood spurted from his nose and he crumpled to the floor, arms trying to shield him from my heels that kicked viciously.

We careened around another curve, lights blinking above the car, a sign whirling by that blared: PLEASE KEEP YOUR SEATS UNTIL COASTER IS AT A FULL STOP!

A platform swung into view with a young man crouched

with a hook. He snagged our car and pulled it to a stop.

"What's the matter?" he demanded, peering down at Fred twisted on the floor, blood staining his coat.

"Nose bleed," I said abruptly. "He'll be okay. Help me get him out."

Fred stood up slowly, his crippled leg bent under him, face red. He staggered onto the platform, worked his cane into position and took my outstretched arm.

"What—what happened?" he muttered, shaking his head, pressing a handkerchief to his nose.

"Is he going to be all right, lady?" the young man asked, forehead ridging.

"Yes," I said. "Where's the nearest phone booth?"

"There's one over by the merry-go-round."

"Thanks."

I helped Fred down a flight of steps and we crossed the night-damp pavement silently, brushing past startled onlookers, until we reached the pay booth.

"Honey, I—I'm bleeding," Fred announced, leaning against the glass doors. "What happened?"

"You tell me, Fred!"

"I—I dunno," he stammered. "Seems to me we were sitting at a bar having a drink and then all of sudden—boom—the lights went out."

"They came on, Fred. They came on. You wait a minute. I've got a call to make."

I stepped inside the booth and deposited a dime in the slot. Then I dialed Mark Storm's office.

"What do you want, Honey?" the lieutenant growled, after he came on the line.

"Did you ever check out any of those people at Sol Wetzel's party?" I demanded.

"Sure, why?"

"What'd they say?"

"They said it was one hell of a shindig. The wildest party they'd been to in a long time. So?"

"So, did anyone mention a tape recorder or any mystic business?"

"Yeah," Mark returned gruffly. "One guy said they held a seance, brought back voices of the dead and that kind of crap. He swore the voices, though, were pre-taped."

I glanced through the glass at Fred's twisted, bloody face. "That's all I wanted to know. Thanks, Lieutenant."

"Thanks for what?" he bellowed. "You're supposed to be in bed."

"I will be," I said, "before the night's over. And sleeping peacefully for a change. See you later, alligator."

I hung up, then dug through the Southern Directory for Rip Spensor's telephone number. A woman's voice answered.

"Who's this?" I demanded.

"Who's this?" she countered.

"Toy?"

"Yes."

"Toy, this is Honey West. Are you alone?"

"Well, no," she stammered. "Ray's here, and my father. What do you want?"

"Listen," I said. "I don't care how you do this, or what excuse you use, but get them both into a car. Drive up to Sol Wetzel's house. I'll meet you there in about an hour."

"But—but I don't understand."

"Something very vital has cropped up in the Angela Scali case," I said. "You won't believe what I've discovered. It's fantastic."

"What is it?"

"I'll explain when I get there. Just do as I say. And remember one thing. Don't let either of them out of your sight for a minute, understand?"

I didn't wait for her answer. Fred gaped at me when I came out of the booth, blood still streaming from his nostrils.

"Honey, what is all this?"

"Fred, do you remember an old saying, 'A dog's bark is worse than his bite?'"

"Sure, but—"

"You keep thinking about that," I said, grasping his hand. "And nothing else. Come on."

It took us about fifteen minutes to walk the six long blocks to my car, Fred hobbling badly on his artificial leg. I didn't bring up Angela Scali again, because I knew it was apt to produce another dire situation with Fred. He sat grimly silent beside me as I drove out the Long Beach Freeway to Hollywood, his jaws clamped tight, eyes staring fixedly in his head.

When we reached Box Canyon, he asked me where we were, but I didn't answer. I kept my hand close to my revolver in readiness for any eventuality. He didn't move. Not even after we pulled up behind Thor Tunny's car parked in Sol Wetzel's driveway.

"Okay," I said, climbing out onto the familiar damp pavement. "Now I want you to do exactly what I tell you to do. Nothing more. Nothing less."

"You've got me, Honey," he said, blinking above the knotted handkerchief he still pressed to his nose.

"Maybe I will thirty minutes from now, Fred. Until then you hold fast, understand? Whatever you see, whatever you hear, try and ignore it. Keep thinking about Bastogne. About the war."

He nodded. "Kind of crazy," he said, perplexedly.

"This is going to be a crazy thirty minutes, Fred." I lifted the reel of tape from the seat, watching his eyes as I took it from under a newspaper.

"What's that?" he demanded.

"I hope it's the answer, Fred. Because if it isn't you're dead."

He followed me to the front door, shuffling awkwardly on his cane. I didn't help. I couldn't erase the events that had occurred in the roller coaster when he'd forced me against the side.

Toy Tunny answered the bell. She was wearing a blue dress and a small hat and looked like she was ready for a wedding, or a funeral. Her father sat in the living room, stiffly erect in his chair, hands clasped over his stomach. He wore the same suit he'd been wearing the night before, with one slight addition. The medallion dangled on his chest, glittering in the light of a table lamp. Ray Spensor stood at the bar, a drink clenched in his fingers, a look of fearful uneasiness creased on his heavy-jawed face.

"I guess you all know Fred Sims," I said, gesturing at the newspaperman.

"What do you want, Miss West." Thor Tunny demanded angrily.

I laughed. "Well, to tell you the truth, I thought maybe we'd have a quiet little seance."

"What?" Ray Spensor broke, leaning away from the bar.

"I'm surprised at your exclamation, Mr. Spensor," I said, shifting my gaze at his reddened face. "I thought sure with your abilities to make things appear and vanish, you'd be the first to shout *hurrah.*"

"Don't be mysterious, Miss West," Toy blurted. "We didn't come here to be entertained."

"Neither did I, Miss Tunny," I said. "But I'm serious about the seance. I'd like to try to bring Sol Wetzel back from the dead."

Ray Spensor jerked, nearly spilling his drink, and choked badly. "Don't be a fool!"

I smiled. "I assure you I'm not. You see, before he died Wetzel wanted to show me something. Something which I'm certain would have explained Angela Scali's murder. I'd like to bring him back for just one moment so that he might tell us what that was."

"Honey," Fred spat, "don't be ridiculous!"

I shrugged, concealing the reel of tape behind my purse. "I'm sure one of you must know how to recall Sol Wetzel. How about you, Mr. Tunny?"

"No!" the cult leader hurled.

"He may even tell the name of his murderer," I said. "How about you, Mr. Spensor?"

"Are you out of your mind?" he returned. "I studied mysticism in Cairo after the war. The senses can create awesome things. This would be insanity."

"Perhaps," I said. "It's worth trying, isn't it?"

"Miss West," Toy added quickly. "I'm afraid you're against a stone wall. You lied to me over the telephone. You have no new information at all. So we'll say good night."

I removed my revolver and leveled it at them. "I'm afraid you won't, Miss Tunny. Draw up a table, Fred. We're having a seance whether they like it or not."

Fred nodded, moved to a round table in the corner and drew it into the center of the room.

"Five chairs, Mr. Spensor," I directed. "And quickly!"

The husky pro football player responded, glancing nervously at Thor Tunny. He pulled five chairs up around the table.

"Now sit," I said.

They sat slowly, eyes fixed on each other, hands resting on the table top. I dimmed the lights and joined them, revolver resting in my lap, tape hidden underneath the gun.

"Who will do the honors?" I asked, surveying their faces.

"I guess I will," Toy broke suddenly. "I'll call for him, but it's futile. You can't bring back the dead when there is any friction or resentment in the room. Sol would never answer."

"Try, Miss Tunny," I said.

"All right," she said, the faint light glowing on her

round cheeks. "Everyone join hands. There must be absolute quiet for at least two minutes."

We joined hands slowly, Toy taking Fred's outstretched fingers, the newsman taking mine. Thor Tunny reached over and caught my right hand grimly, accepting Ray Spensor's in his right. Ray completed the circle by grasping Toy's pudgy left hand. Heavy silence fell over the table. Only the tick of the clock on the mantle made any sound. I kept the tape in my lap with the revolver, both in readiness.

Finally Toy lifted her face up into the dim light and muttered, "Sol? Sol Wetzel? Can you hear me?"

There was no answer. Wind began to whip leaves and branches against the house, brushing ominously.

"Sol Wetzel? I am calling you," she continued tautly. "Can you hear my voice? Can you hear me speaking to you? Come through the barrier. Speak!"

The house creaked. Fred's hand tightened on mine. The clock ticked.

"Solomon Wetzel? I implore you to come forth into this light of lights. To speak," Toy urged. "Tell us what you know of Angela Scali. Tell us what you hold in your hand."

Ray Spensor coughed suddenly, choked it off with a lowering of his head, peered up into the light. Fred sat stiffly immobile at my side.

"It's no use, Miss West," Toy said, shaking her head. "There is too much turbulence in the air."

Thor Tunny said, "Perhaps with the lights extinguished altogether, Miss West."

I stiffened, then rose slowly. "All right. First let me

check the outer bedroom door," I said. "I want to make certain it's unlocked."

"That's a good idea," Tunny said, releasing my hand. I moved across the room, entering the bedroom, fingers still gripped around the spool and my revolver. I knew I had to work quickly, and in the dark. I crossed to where I'd left the tape recorder and no sooner had the tape threaded on the machine when I heard a sound coming from the living room. I froze in my tracks.

"I am here!" a voice cried, lifting resonantly.

I raced back to the door and saw Fred Sims standing upright in the dim light, his face pale and twisted.

"My God," he whispered, "it—it's Angela!"

The voice seemed to rise out of thin air above the table. "Frederic, my love!"

"Speak to me, Angela," Fred urged breathlessly. Tears began to stream down his cheeks.

"Someone has been calling, Fred," the voice floated. "Sol cannot hear you as I can. Speak!"

I gripped the edge of the door, hair rising on the back of my neck, as I stared into the room at the four frozen people.

"Angela," Fred cried. "She made me do it. I couldn't help myself."

"Who, Fred?" the voice demanded.

The table suddenly overturned, Thor Tunny tumbling to the floor, Ray Spensor falling backward.

I saw her rise in the contorted light, flick open her thick-lipped mouth, scream in pathetic horrifying gasps of despair.

"Angel!" Toy screamed. "Angel! I didn't mean to, believe me!"

She whirled toward the door, but Fred swung his cane furiously in the air, striking the pudgy girl and knocking her to the floor.

Toy rolled over, choking, half-screaming, "Kill her, Fred! Kill her!"

Fred's cane thudded ruthlessly on Toy Tunny's head, until the force of his hate was spent, and he stood over her, his face twisted his shoulders shaking with choking sobs.

SEVENTEEN

"She'll live," Mark said, as he came down the hospital corridor, face deeply lined, hat twisted in his big hands.

He thrust his elbows on the nurse's reception desk and stared at me, an unlighted cigarette dangling from his lips.

"She lost a lot of blood," he added.

I winced. "Now you know what almost happened to me."

The deputy clenched his teeth. "Yeah. Let's get a cup of coffee."

We found a diet kitchen, along one of the back corridors, where a pot of coffee was brewing on the stove. Mark poured us each a cup and settled heavily into a chair.

"Fred Sims," he said softly, chewing on his knuckles. "My God."

"I tried to warn you, Mark," I said, leaning against the corner and exhaling hard.

"Why didn't he tell us he was married to the Italian Angel? Why did he help her disappear?"

"Love works in devious ways, Lieutenant. He couldn't help himself."

"Yeah, but fifteen years later," Mark said, almost to himself.

"You'll have to go back farther than that," I said. "Fred's from a broken home. He spent a lot of time alone as a kid. Most of it brooding, depressed. That was probably what made him a hero at Bastogne. Up until that time he hadn't had much to live for."

"So he lost a leg in Germany," Mark roared. "That didn't wreck him completely."

"No, but it deepened his neurosis. Made him withdraw even farther from society. Fred's a lonely man, Mark. Lonely men do only two things. Drink and die."

The deputy rubbed his forehead with the flat of his hand, peering up at me. "Where'd you read that, in one of Fred's columns?"

"No, I think it was someplace in Hemingway. Fred was a target, Mark. A man displaced. Like Adam Jason. Their thoughts and beliefs were all tangled together."

Mark got to his feet, shoving his cup on the counter. "I feel like getting drunk—and don't tell me I'm a lonely man."

"There's a bottle in my office," I said. "You want to join a lonely woman?"

"Why not?"

We walked outside into a lemon-colored dawn that stretched like silk across a cloud-clear sky. The unplayed tape lay on the front seat of my convertible.

"What's that?" Mark demanded.

"A bit of undigested evidence," I said. "Before I had a chance to play it for our cast of characters, Angela Scali interrupted with her curtain speech."

"I still don't get that bit of hocus-pocus," the deputy said, watching me shift the car into low, moving us out of the hospital's parking lot. "The Angel's in the County Morgue."

"Of course, she is. But somebody took the liberty of resurrecting her. At least, for the moment."

"Who?"

"Thor Tunny. He'd been a carney man in his early days. Done everything from voice imitations to ventriloquism. He had his suspicions. His performance last night really electrified our murderer."

"I can imagine. But what's on the tape?"

"It's sort of Sol Wetzel's last will and testament. I thought we'd listen to it while we had our drink."

Mark nodded dismally. "Okay, by me."

Lights still blazed along downtown streets as we turned into the parking lot behind my office. Dawn cut the sky deeper and wider. We crossed the asphalt slowly, shoes clattering. Upstairs behind the frosted glass door that read: H. WEST, PRIVATE INVESTIGATOR, I poured two drinks, then spooled the tape onto my recorder. I ran it back to the beginning and reversed the reel.

"I made a mistake night before last," I said. "Not realizing this was the *front half* of a broken tape I played it and got nothing. That was because I forgot that a split reel placed on the other spindle plays the opposite side."

"So what does that prove?" Mark asked, sipping at his drink.

"You told me that you checked out some of Sol Wetzel's party-goers. One of them said he thought some of the hi-jinx was pre-taped. Well, this I believe is the tape."

I pressed the PLAY button and a voice laughed, "Hey, that's fun. Why not try it on Sol?"

Other voices shouted, "'Yes! Good idea! Make Sol sweat!"

"Not me," Sol Wetzel's voice floated up. "I don't like that kind of stuff. Let's play strip poker instead."

"No!" argued another. "Put Sol under. Make him confess his sins!"

"Okay," Wetzel said. "But you'll all be sorry."

There came a general rush of laughter, then footsteps clattered.

"Where do you want me to sit?"

"Here," a woman said. "In the light."

Mark's forehead ridged. "That sounds like Toy Tunny."

"It is," I said.

Toy's voice continued, "You feel very tired, Sol. Relax all your muscles and imagine you are going into a deep sleep. Look up into the light. Keep looking at it. Just relax. That's better. You feel yourself drifting. Falling sound, sound asleep. Deeper and deeper and deeper."

Mark got to his feet. "She's hypnotizing him."

"That's right," I said.

"You're sleeping now, Sol," Toy continued monotonously. "A deep sleep. One that is becoming deeper and deeper. A pleasant sleep."

Laughter broke, died. Mark's eyes studied the turning reels intently.

"When you wake, Sol," Toy's voice droned, "you will not be as peaceful. You will be angry. Your worst enemy will be standing near you, even though you won't be able to see him. He's come to harm you, Sol. Do you understand? He's got a gun and he's threatening you with it."

"No!" Sol Wetzel's voice exploded.

Toy's tone lowered. "But you're not afraid, Sol. Not at first. Tell him what you think of him, but look out for his gun."

After a long moment of silence, Wetzel's voice lifted, "You fool! You think you're smart, don't you? Well, you're not. You're a fool!"

Mark straightened, shooting a narrow-eyed glance at me.

"I'll kill you!" Wetzel's voice rose defiantly. "If you come closer, I'll kill you!"

"But, that's—" Mark stammered, staring at the whirling reels.

"No!" Wetzel cried. "No! No! No!"

The tape jerked off the end of the spool and spun, clicking harshly on the half-filled reel. Mark advanced toward the recorder, eyes wide.

"But, Honey," he protested. "That's exactly what you told me Wetzel said just before he died."

"That's correct, Lieutenant," I said, shutting off the machine. "There's concrete evidence. Wetzel was dead long before I ever entered that room."

"But I thought—"

"What, that Fred killed him? Don't be ridiculous, Mark! Fred was only a post-hypnotic pawn along Toy Tunny's vengeful road to murder. She killed them all. Rip Spensor, Angela Scali, Sol Wetzel—and indirectly Adam Jason."

EIGHTEEN

Mark opened the cell door and stared in at Fred Sims, who was hunched forward on a bunk, head in his hands.

"Come on out, killer," the deputy said lowly.

"Leave me alone," the newspaperman murmured. "Just leave me alone."

"Honey and I have something to tell you, Fred."

"I don't want to hear it."

"This might make good front page copy."

"Yeah," Fred mumbled, staring at us in the dim light. "Like reporter goes berserk? Makes up for lives he saved during war? And that's all he wrote."

"Not all, Fred," I added. "Come on, we want to show you something."

He shrugged, lifted on his cane and went into Mark's office with us. I showed him a book on hypnotism.

"Ever read anything on this subject?" I asked.

"No."

"Do you know what a post-hypnotic suggestion is?"

"Vaguely," Fred answered, brushing at his face.

I dropped the book on Mark's desk and said, "Well, until you struck Toy Tunny down you were under a pretty severe one. Severe enough to kill under the right stimuli."

"I—I don't get you."

"Didn't you tell me, Fred, that on the day of Angela's death you underwent two periods of mental blackout?"

"Yes."

"The first occurred after you found Angela's body hanging from the tree, isn't that so?"

"Yes, but—"

"What was your reaction upon making that discovery?"

Fred slumped into a chair, face contorted. "I—I cried like a baby. I thought my insides would drop out. It was the worst moment of my life. Then everything went blank."

"Did you remember that she was dead when you came to in her shower stall?"

"No," Fred blurted. "No, I didn't."

"Probably temporary amnesia," I said, looking at Mark. "The impact must have thrown him for a loop." I studied Fred again. "Then you didn't remember her death when you drove to my apartment later that same morning?"

"No."

"Nor when you returned with me to Meadow Falls?"

The newspaperman shook his head dazedly. "I—I didn't remember until Mark came into the temple and said he'd found her by the falls. Then—then I knew I'd killed her."

"Why, Fred?"

"Because I recalled washing her blood off my suit. I remembered reaching up for her."

"But you also said you had the recollection of finding her already dead. Didn't that mean anything to you?"

"Of course. But somehow I couldn't believe it. Not until after I talked with Toy."

"When did this conversation occur, Fred?"

"In Thor Tunny's office, shortly before the other blackout."

"Do you recall what was said?"

"Some of it. Toy told me she thought she knew who had murdered Angela. I became very frightened. Sick to my stomach. I laid down on the couch, and—"

"And what, Fred?"

"Then—then—"

"You went blank again."

"Yes."

"I'll tell you what happened, Fred. Toy hypnotized you."

"What?"

"She convinced you that I killed Angela Scali. She even went further and suggested that until I was dead you'd never have a moment's peace."

"But that's fantastic, Honey," Fred protested.

"Not half so fantastic as your attacks upon me in the mountain cabin, the gate shack and again on the roller coaster. Your subconscious was convinced of my guilt. And not until Toy screamed for forgiveness for Angela's death in Sol Wetzel's living room was the spell broken."

"Honey, you mean Toy Tunny killed Angela?"

I nodded.

"How about Spensor?"

"Spensor and Wetzel. Jason committed suicide, but obviously through her influence."

"I thought—"

"Sure you did," I said. "Toy inflicted you with that thought. The same as she did with Adam Jason. He was so convinced of his own guilt he even wrote out a confession."

"But how did she do it, Honey? And why?"

"Sol Wetzel denied he was ever in love with Angela. But he said he knew of someone who was in love with her. That was the key to the whole case." I took a diary from my purse and tossed it on Mark's desk. "I found this in Toy's handbag. It belongs to Wetzel, and apparently is the object he was looking for when he went into his bedroom. It tells of a mixed-up love triangle between Toy Tunny, Rip Spensor and Angela Scali."

Fred jerked to his feet. "What?"

"Wetzel says in his diary that Toy was deeply in love with Rip Spensor. So was Angela. To Rip, both love affairs were a sometimes pleasurable game that he kept going for the fun of it. Apparently Toy found out about Rip's association with Angela and me, and her evil little mind began creating all sorts of pictures. She must have decided if she couldn't have Rip Spensor, no one could. So she plotted the destruction of Angela, Spensor and me."

"Incredible," Fred murmured.

"At first Toy must have figured on Angela being

accused of murdering Rip and me. But she didn't count on my escaping the tarantulas. Nor Angela coming to me."

"Where'd the tarantulas come from?"

"From a cage buried in Rip's backyard. Adam probably stole them, at Toy's hypnotic command, and then placed them in my car."

Mark lifted a shade behind his desk, allowing light to flood into the room. Fred blinked, shaking his head dazedly.

"It might clarify things if you start at the beginning, Honey," the deputy suggested. "With Rip Sensor."

"Okay," I said. "That night, following the Rams-Forty-niners game, Angela had a rendezvous with Rip at his house. Toy followed her, no doubt spying on their movements inside the house. After Angela drove away, Toy slammed the steam roller into high gear and caught Rip flat-footed on the road."

"But Angela," Fred blurted. "How could Toy have lifted her up onto that tree branch?"

"She didn't," I said. "You remember the wind was blowing quite violently that morning just before the storm broke. Toy must have stabbed Angela by the mountain stream. Then when one of those tree branches was blown close to her, she caught it with a rope, tied a noose and slipped it around the Angel's neck. Then she let the limb spring back into place."

"But why Sol Wetzel?" Fred asked, regarding me tautly with his steel-grey eyes.

"As I explained. Wetzel said he had something to show me. Toy must have become frightened when he showed her the diary while I waited outside the bedroom. Not realizing what was going on I switched on the radio. Unfortunately, the sound drowned out any sound of murder. Then Toy played the tape of Wetzel's speech, which provided her with an alibi."

"How'd you figure that one, Honey?" Mark asked, shaking his head.

"First, I believed Ray Spensor when he said he'd heard no one come down that walkway behind Wetzel's house. Secondly, I couldn't find the other reel of that broken tape."

"So that brings us to Adam Jason," the deputy said.

"Yes, Adam was one of Toy's hypnotic pawns. For a second time she sent him to murder me, but Adam apparently couldn't go through with it. Instead he took the poison that was meant for me and that was finis for him—and Toy Tunny.

"You see, Fred," I continued. "Under hypnotic suggestion a person will not commit an act or crime which is against his will or morals normally. In your case, on the other hand, the burning love you felt for Angela drove you to violent hatred toward her murderer. For you, a person who was forced to kill again and again during the war, murder to avenge the death of your love was an automatic thing."

Fred got up slowly and hobbled to the window. He stared out at the new day and at the city that was beginning to stretch in the morning sunshine. Then he groaned.

"What about Toy Tunny?" the newsman asked.

"She's going to live," Mark said. "At least until she reaches the gas chamber."

"You mean—I'm free to go?"

"Not quite," I said. "There's one thing we haven't disposed of."

"What's that?"

"My brakeless ride down the mountain. Who slipped me the brass ring?"

"I—I don't know," Fred stammered.

"You were driving the car. Didn't you notice anything wrong with the brakes?"

"No."

"Where'd you park the car after you returned to the camp?"

"Behind the temple."

"Were the keys in it?"

"Yes," Fred answered, after a moment.

"Must have been Adam Jason," I said. "Under Toy's spell he probably figured I'd try to escape in that car while they were hunting for me. Poor Adam. He was under the same sort of hypnotic trance that you were Fred. Toy had you both eating out of her hand."

"Remind me never to look anybody straight in the eyes again," Fred managed, brushing at his brows.

I smiled. "And remind me never to take a roller coaster ride without a parachute."

"I—I'm sorry, Honey."

I patted his cheek. "Well, I'm not. If you hadn't jumped me the way you did I probably never would have figured Toy Tunny. Worse, you might have killed yourself as Jason did."

Mark Storm got to his feet, stretched and wrapped

his thick arms about my neck. "How about you and me taking a little ride."

"Where to, Lieutenant?" I said slyly.

"Into orbit."

"Okay," I said.

We started for the door. Fred's voice stopped us.

"She's got you in a trance, Marcus," the reporter said, grinning.

Mark grinned back. "Good," he said. "It's just about my turn, isn't it?"

Outside in the corridor, he shoved me against the wall and kissed me.

"You feel very tired, Lieutenant," I whispered in his ear. "Very, very tired. You are going into a deep sleep. Deeper and deeper. Your eyelids are heavy."

He lifted me into his arms.

"You have me in your power," he said. "What is your command."

"Take me to your launching pad, commander!"

"Aye, aye, sir."

We staggered down the steps to the street. I smiled up at him. Next stop. The moon!